Mr. Hass
Muirz joi
gone near

Doctor Englaster spoke with sarcasm. "Really, you take longer to weave your spells nowadays, don't you?"

Miss Muirz shrugged. "I weave well-made goods, Doctor."

"So I have heard."

Watch out, Doc, Mr. Hassam thought, watch what you say to her. She is not a patient soul like I am and if she should get her fill of you, then you are likely to be in trouble.

"How did Mr. Harsh impress you, Miss Muirz?" Mr. Hassam spoke hastily.

"Perfect."

"How did you get along with him? Can he be handled?"

"I think so. He reacts normally. I gave him an overdose of sex, followed by an overdose of culture—in other words, I waved my bottom at him, then read to him aloud from Spinoza. Yes, I would say he reacts normally."

Mr. Hassam considered the combination of Miss Muirz's bottom and Spinoza, and he wondered how Harsh had survived.

Doctor Englaster spoke sharply. "And you think this man will do for our purpose?"

"Perfectly." There was a strange look in Miss Muirz's eyes. "He even has El Presidente's dirtily eager way with women..."

HONEY *in* *his* MOUTH

by **Lester Dent**

A HARD CASE CRIME NOVEL

A HARD CASE CRIME BOOK

(HCC-060)

First Hard Case Crime edition: October 2009

Published by

Titan Books
A division of Titan Publishing Group Ltd
144 Southwark Street
London SE1 0UP

in collaboration with Winterfall LLC

Print edition ISBN 978-0-85768-329-8
E-book ISBN 978-0-85768-401-1

Cover design by Cooley Design Lab
Design direction by Max Phillips
Typeset by Swordsmith Productions

Printed in the United States of America

Visit us on the web at www.HardCaseCrime.com

HONEY IN HIS MOUTH

PART ONE

ONE

He should have paid the bill. But who would have thought that some afternoon he would drive into a filling station and there would be D. C. Roebuck standing by a gas pump? He saw that Roebuck was holding up five fingers to the attendant and could hear Roebuck's harsh voice, like glass being chewed: "Five regular, Mac. And check the oil."

Walter Harsh did the only thing he could think of, sit there with hands on the steering wheel, foot on the brake, a mouse nest gathering in the pit of his stomach. He wished he had not talked D. C. Roebuck into letting him have seven hundred and twelve dollars worth of photographic supplies on tick. Mostly he wished to hell and gone that he had not run into D. C. Roebuck.

It came to him that just sitting there in the parked car he was a sitting duck. He eased the gear shift into drive position and pressed the gas pedal with his foot. Just then Roebuck turned and saw him. "Hey!"

Walter Harsh pushed the gas pedal to the floor.

Roebuck leaped over the gas hose and ran forward. "Hold it, Harsh! I want to see you, you son of a bitch. Hold it!"

Harsh did not look around. The cushion felt like a big hand pressing against his spine as the car gained speed. He almost didn't make it at that. Roebuck overtook the car, but he couldn't find anything to grab with his hands. Harsh heard Roebuck's hands clawing at the car. Then there was a thud. When he turned his head for a quick look, he saw the big man had hit the back window an angry blow with his fist. It had cracked the window glass. He saw Roebuck back in the street floundering the way a big man flops around when he tries to stop running abruptly, and he heard what Roebuck shouted. "I'll fix you. Thieving bastard, I'll fix you good." Roebuck stopped, turned, ran toward his own car.

The filling station was on the north edge of a small Missouri town named Carrollton. The sun was shining on the concrete highway. There was a ridge of snow mixed with dirt along the shoulder on each side of the pavement where the highway plow had pushed it. There was some snow in the fields with weeds and corn stalks sticking out of it.

Harsh's car went faster and faster, passing several signs in fields. *Thank You*, one sign said. *Come again to Carrollton, Missouri*, the second said. *God Bless You, the Carrollton Baptist Church*, said the third sign. The rear-view mirror was a little off. He reached up and adjusted it and saw Roebuck's car swing into view, following him. Well, that ties it, he thought, the big guy is going to give me trouble.

He veered to the center of the highway to get a full swing at a curve he saw ahead, figuring that way he could go into the curve ten miles an hour faster. There was some howling from the tires in the curve. When he straightened out, he looked back, saw Roebuck seemed to be gaining on him already.

They were headed north. The highway went straight for a while, but with ups and downs over the hills. He began to wonder, suppose he couldn't outrun Roebuck, what he was going to do? There was no use to try to talk the man out of anything. Talk was what Roebuck had already heard. Talk was what had cost Roebuck seven hundred and twelve dollars. The company had forced Roebuck to make the bad credit good out of his own pocket. He had told Harsh about this in a bar in St. Joseph, and Harsh had said he thought Roebuck was a damn fool for working for that kind of a company, which was when Roebuck grabbed a bottle off the display on the backbar. Roebuck was an enormous man with long powerful arms, a bad-tempered man. He chased Harsh out of the bar and for two terrifying blocks before Harsh outdistanced him. It had been a shattering experience. The man would have killed him.

Roebuck was gaining, all right.

Harsh reached down and punched the choke button with the ball of his thumb to make sure the choke was not pulled out. His car engine was cold-blooded these winter days and had to be choked before it would start; sometimes he forgot and left the choke out. He thought of something and eased the choke back out a little to enrich the mixture to see if that would add any speed. The speedometer dropped from ninety-five to ninety. He pushed the choke back in. He couldn't think of anything more to do. The old heap just didn't have it. Put off the valve job too long, he thought.

On a road as straight as this it did not help a man to be a skillful driver. Any fool could tramp the gas and tool down the middle of the road. A crossroads snapped past. What about trying to make it into the next crossroads, he wondered, and take off down some country road. Try to lose Roebuck that way. Oh sure, he thought, let the son of a bitch catch me on a lonely back road and he'll kill me sure.

The car behind continued to gain on him.

He gripped the steering wheel and kept the gas pressed down with all the strength in his foot. He saw now what he should have done was stay put in the service station—that way there would have been a witness handy when Roebuck jumped him. He had seen one man around the filling station, a tall fellow with pale curly hair, who would have been a witness. One witness was better than none.

Roebuck's car was about three hundred feet behind.

Harsh was not panic-stricken, he did not think he was going to pieces or anything, but he knew there was real danger from Roebuck. He remembered Vera Sue had said Roebuck was dangerous. "Walter, I know you're fixing to screw Mr. Roebuck, and I wish you wouldn't. He gets real wild when he's excited, real awfully wild. I am afraid you'll wish you hadn't messed with him." Vera Sue Crosby was Harsh's business associate and she had lent him a little help, at his suggestion, in suckering Roebuck. "Walter, the guy goes nuts, you get him excited." At the time, Harsh had laughed because he knew that being in a hotel room with Vera Sue would make most fellows rattle their marbles.

One hundred feet behind.

Harsh supposed that using the girl to con Roebuck out of seven hundred and twelve dollars worth of photo supplies was what had driven the man crazy. If Harsh had stuck to the straight con and left out sex, maybe Roebuck wouldn't have blown his top. However it made no difference now, it was water past the bridge. Harsh had used the photo supplies. He did not have money to pay up. All he could do was run for it. The roar from his engine was deafening and the whole car pounded and shuddered. Son of a bitch trying to fly to pieces, he thought.

The chase was beginning to look like a matter of time, time and providence. If they would only pass a highway cop. But he knew they wouldn't. When you needed a highway cop they were always gassing a waitress in a restaurant. If he hadn't been fleeing for his life, if he'd been burning up the highway at ninety-five just for kicks, a cop would be popping from behind every fencepost. That was the way it went, he thought, the potlickers never around when you wanted them.

Fifty feet.

He glanced over the inside of his car looking for something he could use for a weapon to defend himself. In the front seat there was nothing. The only loose objects in the back seat were his camera in its case and the tripod, but the tripod was strapped tight to the camera case, and he knew from experience it would not be easy to unstrap it at this speed. The camera had cost too much money to use it for a weapon. Bust it all to hell, he thought, if I go banging it on that bird's thick skull. Traveling at this speed he wondered if he dared fool around unstrapping the tripod. It was not very heavy anyway, not much use if he did get it loose. The car took another curve, not much of a curve, but the tires skidded and gave out high girl-like shrieks. Coming out of the curve the speedometer read ninety miles and it quickly climbed to ninety-seven.

When the roar of passing air began to have a different quality, he knew what caused it before he swung his head to look. Roebuck was pulling abreast in the left lane.

"Hey, Harsh! Stop your car!" Roebuck had rolled down

his right-hand window. "You want me to knock you off the road?" He sounded as if he was chewing rocks now.

"Get away from me," Harsh shouted. The road ahead lay straight over rolling hills. "Let me alone!"

The cars touched, bounced, wobbled. Harsh brought his machine under control readily enough. He was afraid to hit the brakes because at this speed no telling if it would throw the car off the road. They sped on, the other car drawing up slowly until it was nearly abreast. His throat felt tight. Let the other car get far enough ahead, nudge his front wheel, and he was a goner. He threw a look at Roebuck. The man was steering with just his left hand on the wheel, and there was a metal object in his right. Roebuck's thick body began squirming toward the middle of the seat. The metal object was a small hydraulic jack weighing about twenty pounds, and he was going to hurl it at Harsh's head. Oh Jesus, Harsh thought, and he threw up his left hand to fend off the jack. But the windstream struck his arm a blow, driving the arm back and actually causing his hand to bang against the outside of his car.

At that moment the cars came together. The impact did not seem violent. A gentle kiss of heavy metal bodies. But Harsh's left hand was hanging out between the cars and his arm was broken. The ends of the bones appeared through the cloth of his coat sleeve like two large fangs.

Roebuck's car swerved left and the outside pair of wheels dropped off the slab. Both machines were going downhill, speed slightly over 100 mph. Roebuck's car hooked into the snow, slewed over and collided with a concrete culvert. The culvert wall, reinforced concrete three feet high, a foot thick, nearly fifteen feet long, sliced through Roebuck's car like a hatchet through a shoebox. What was left of the car went end over end, hitting and bouncing, hitting and bouncing, landing on Roebuck's body the third hit, passing through a barbed wire fence and rolling about one hundred feet further into a bean stubblefield. A large cloud of snow and loose earth accompanied it into the stubblefield.

Harsh did not know he was injured until he noticed his left arm was still hanging out the window, and he started to draw it back. He almost screamed from the pain. He looked at the arm, the grayish bone ends sticking through the cloth of his sleeve. He found he had no control of the arm from the shoulder down. He felt a warm slippery quality in his trousers, decided he had shit his pants. He cursed his luck, his carelessness, his stupidity. The arm had been between the cars when they came together, he thought, and it was busted all to hell.

He cut his speed down to about twenty, which seemed awfully slow by comparison, almost as if he could step out and walk faster. He wondered, should he go back and learn how Roebuck had fared. Maybe the man needed help. He could work up no enthusiasm for this idea, however. He really should get his arm back inside the car, he thought. Wonder how bunged it was, bad as it looked? To be safe he had better stop the car. He did so, but did not pull over on the shoulder because of the snow. There was no traffic in view anyway. He reached over, gritted his teeth, took hold of his left arm with his right hand. Oh God! He almost passed out. Then he was sick and his arm hurt so he could not put his head out of the window, resulting in his making a mess inside his car.

Presently he felt some better, and wiped the tears out

of his eyes. Better get the damn arm in, give it one big jerk if no other way. Suddenly he seized the mangled arm and yanked it back into the car. Then his head bent back and he screamed several times. He couldn't help it.

Well, the arm was in the car, and now he should get to a hospital probably. That was the ticket, a hospital. He shoved the gear shift into forward drive and fed the gas slowly so as not to jerk the car and hurt his arm. The machine rolled quietly, and driving was not as much work as he had feared. Damn car, he thought, runs like a baby now. Turned into an old man when it mattered. Trade the son of a bitch off, he thought, first chance I get. Swap it for a mule, if he had to. He looked down at his lap and saw a pool of blood from his arm. This scared him, for he had heard a man could bleed to death and never know it. He watched the arm closely, between keeping his eyes on the road, but the blood pool did not seem to be growing. He was going to make it, he decided.

He crossed a bridge over a small river and saw a series of billboards, which meant a town. He would keep his eye open for some building that looked like a hospital. He could not see any buildings extending above treetop level. A hospital worthy of the name would be higher than the treetops, he felt, and he began to suspect this was a jerk town that didn't have a decent hospital. Another thing: The way Roebuck's car had gone end over end, he felt Roebuck had been killed for sure. What if someone had seen his car give D. C. Roebuck's car the nudge that sent it stem-winding into the bean field? Had anyone been watching? He tried to remember. He decided that as fast as he had been traveling and the rest of it, he wouldn't have noticed the U.S. Marine Corps if they had been lined up in dress parade along the highway. *Can't stop in this town. I better keep going far enough nobody will connect me with Roebuck*. He decided he felt up to going on.

So he did not turn off the highway as he had planned. There was no stop sign, only a SLOW, which he observed carefully, then drove on. He could make it somewhere. Make it, hell, he thought, he could drive a hundred miles if he had to. Maybe a couple hundred would be better.

Presently he decided he could use a smoke. He felt out the pack of cigarettes in his shirt pocket and pulled forth one cigarette. He had to bend forward to reach the lighter on the dash and when he did, his left arm slid off his lap down into the narrow space between the left side of the seat and the car door. The pain pried his mouth open as if invisible hands had wrenched at his jaw.

As he had reached for the lighter, in the moment before pain paralyzed him, he noticed blood on the carpet. He looked down again. The cigarette had fallen from his lips, was lying in a pool of blood on the floor. He stretched out his left leg and saw the cloth was soaked with red. The arm, unknown to him, had been bleeding down the trouser leg. He became frightened again. What if he passed out and the car went off the road? That would fix him, wouldn't it?

TWO

It was late afternoon when Walter Harsh's car turned into a service station across from a chicken hatchery in a small water tower town in northeast Missouri. A bell gave a *ping* when the wheels ran over a rubber hose, the car stopped, an attendant came out and dipped a sponge in a bucket of water. He took his time squeezing excess water from the sponge. He began to swab the windshield.

"Tell me, Jack, you got a good doctor in this town?" Harsh was not completely sure that the car had stopped moving. Pain made everything look as if it had a short red fuzz growing on it.

The attendant misunderstood. "How many gallons was that?" He rubbed at the windshield. His neck stiffened a little. He had smelled the vomit inside the car.

Harsh was completely confused by receiving a question in answer to what he recalled was a question the way he asked it. What had he asked the bird anyway? Ain't in no shape to figure something out, he thought. But he was very scared inside, and being scared caused him to wish to be agreeable, so he smiled. It felt as if a hook had fastened under his upper lip and was dragging it up against his nose.

"How many you say, sir?"

Harsh could not think what he was doing here. Something to do with a damn building that would not stick up above the trees.

The attendant finished the passenger side of the windshield and walked around to the other. He saw blood on the side of the car, and there was a faint whistling sound as his breath left him.

"Holy Moses, Mister. What's this stuff all over the side of your car?" The attendant bent down and peered, put the end of a finger in the blood, which was coagulated and about like gravy. "Holy Moses!" He ran into the service station and seized the telephone. "Flo, this is Jiggs. Get Doc over here in a hurry. Got a man here bled near to death." The attendant now had a high thin voice. The telephone fell to the floor when he tried to put it back on the desk. He let it lie. He ran out for another look at the man in the car. "Harold! Harold!" He ran across the street to the chicken hatchery. Soon he came back with Harold, a stocky alert-eyed man. Harold said not to move the victim, never move an accident victim, and was Doc coming?

Harsh did not bother to comment. Lot of silly rummies, running around hollering, like chickens that had jumped out of that place across the street.

He closed his eyes, didn't open them again till he heard another car squeal to a stop ten feet away, then a man's voice. "What have you here, Jiggs?"

"Doc, I think he was shot. I didn't touch him."

Doc had the gaunt frame of an Abe Lincoln and the lazy movements and drawl of a cane-pole fisherman. "Jiggs, you better call Kenny Wilson for his ambulance."

"Sure, Doc."

A hypodermic needle was waved near Harsh's face. "This won't hurt. And you are going to be all right."

Sure he was all right, Harsh thought, he was fine, they could fart around all day.

°

He was on a cart. A fat man in a white suit pushed him
along between white walls under a beige ceiling. A nurse
walked alongside, wiping the sweat off his forehead and
from around his eyes. He was pushed into a room and the
attendant left but the nurse stayed. Presently the doctor
came in and stood looking at him.

"Feeling fine, eh?"

"You want the truth, Doc, I feel like I ain't all here."

The doctor got out a stethoscope, stuck the prongs in
his ears and listened to Harsh's chest. "You have a heart
like a horse."

"A galloping horse, maybe. What's the matter with it?"

"It's okay. How does your arm feel?"

"Feel? I don't feel nothing." They had cut off his arm,
he decided. He was afraid to feel or even look to make
sure, yet he wanted very much to know.

The doctor smoked a cigarette. He put his foot on a
chair and knocked the cigarette ash into his trouser cuff.
The room was soundless, but there was plenty of noise in
the hallways. The bed smelled faintly of stuff they had
put in the sheets to sterilize them.

"Tell me, Doc."

"Yes?"

"My left arm, where did you cut it off?"

The doctor laughed as if someone had cracked a huge
joke. "My lord, man. Your arm is full of medication, is all.
You're not going to lose the arm."

"Oh. It didn't feel as if it was there." He felt good
about the arm, and asked the doctor for a cigarette. The
first puff made him sick and he tried to heave and his left

arm hurt as though lightning had struck it. "Jesus God! What did you do to it?"

"Set it." The doctor waited for the attack of pain to subside. "The arm was badly broken. But listen, the arm's not the thing. Here's the thing: Did you know you have O-negative blood?"

"What?"

"You have O-negative blood. Rather rare around here —only seven people out of a hundred have it. Do you know anybody we can get hold of who does? Any blood relatives in these parts?"

"Doc, I didn't know there was such a thing as O-negative blood, whatever it is."

"Well, you need a blood transfusion, Harsh, and we have no O-negative in our blood bank. If you know anybody that we can reach who has it, you had better tell me."

"I can't help you, Doc. How about just any old blood?"

The doctor shook his head. "If you've got O-negative, you can't take any other type. It could kill you." A heavy, white-haired, middle-aged nurse came into the room. She said she had been on the telephone to the Red Cross and learned they had an O-negative donor listed in a nearby town. He was a mechanic and was out at somebody's farm fixing a tractor, but the police were sending a car over to bring him in. The doctor turned to Harsh. "You're a lucky man, Harsh. I guess we'll be able to get you fixed up." But Harsh was asleep.

It was morning. He was lying on a hospital bed as naked as a jaybird under the sheet. The doctor came in and yanked back the sheet and pressed thoughtfully on his body with fingertips, then drew the sheet up to his chin.

"You're feeling great, my boy."

"That is one hell of an overstatement, Doc. What did you do to me?"

"The donor got here, that mechanic. You're full of his blood now and good as new." The doctor took a chart off a hook at the foot of the bed, looked at it, and put it back on the hook. "By the way, Harsh, there's a city policeman out front. I'll bring him in, so you can thank him for getting that blood donor up here for you."

"Tell you the truth, Doc, I feel too sick to be seeing any cop."

"Nonsense. You're not that bad off."

The doctor turned and went out. As soon as he had gone, Harsh tried to get out of bed. He did not want to talk to a police officer. But weakness seized him and he had to flop back on the bed and lie helpless. The blood out of that grease monkey, he thought, didn't have much strength in it.

The policeman threw the door wide and came in. He was a big man with a bald head and an unfriendly manner, and it was immediately clear he was interested in getting more than thanks. He listened while Harsh said he understood the police had hunted up the blood donor, and thanks. Thanks a lot. Harsh wanted to get rid of him, and he was very polite.

"No sweat at all, fellow. Line of duty." The officer got out a notebook. "Now, about that arm. What happened to it?"

"Well, a car sideswiped me, officer. Like I put in the report."

"What report?"

"Hey! Say now, I guess I didn't get around to that. Tell you the truth, I was in pretty bad shape. All the time I remember thinking, my arm is all smashed to hell, I got to get to a Doc, and I got to report this like the law says."

"So those were sideswipe marks on your car?"

"Tell you the truth, officer, I wouldn't know if my car was marked up or not. With this arm the way it was, I just couldn't get up the steam to notice anything else."

"How did it happen?"

"I had my elbow out the open window, the way a fellow drives along. Then like I say, here comes some bird and sideswipes me. You know something, officer, for a while there I didn't even know I was hurt."

"You remember anything about the car?"

"I couldn't swear, but I think it was a green Chevy, this year's model, a four-door, I think. The guy, he was in it all by himself, a smallish guy with a dark face, and he was wearing a tan cap. You know, that's about all I remember. Maybe it was my fault. Maybe I was crowding the center line."

"When it happened, didn't the other car stop?"

"Not that I saw. He high-tailed it right on down the road."

"Where was this?"

"Officer, I wish I could tell you for exact sure, but it was south of the Iowa line a little ways, is the best I can do."

The officer took a bite at the end of his pencil. "Your correct name is Walter Harsh. You're from Hollywood, California. Right?"

"No. I don't know where you got your information about me, officer, but I ain't from Hollywood, California. I'm from Quincy, Illinois. Say now, wait—I'm the president of National Studios of Hollywood, that must have given you the idea I'm from Hollywood, California."

"The National Studios of Hollywood, eh?"

"You got it."

The officer put this down in his notebook. "But your name *is* Walter Harsh?"

"Yes."

"All right. Now what is the address in Hollywood of this National Studios?"

"You're mixed up, officer. There ain't any address in Hollywood. The address of National Studios of Hollywood is in Quincy, Illinois, the same as my address."

"Oh."

"I hope you got it right now, officer."

The policeman pulled a chair to the bedside and put one foot on it to make a desk for his notebook. "Harsh, are you a movie guy?"

"Motion pictures? Me? Oh brother, did you miss it again."

"Well, what are you?"

"I'm nothing but a photo drummer."

"What is that?"

"I take pictures of people house-to-house. Which reminds me, officer, in my car. My box. I mean my camera, did you notice was it still in my car?"

"The hospital people had your camera and suitcase brought in and put with your other stuff in a locker here at the hospital."

"Say, that's all right. I was afraid somebody would make off with it. That camera set me back."

The policeman's eyes were not leaving Harsh. The creases in his uniform were very neat, as if this was the first time he had worn the uniform. There was the faint smell of gun oil about him, and his brass and leather were shiny.

"Now, Harsh, let's get one more thing. Who do we notify at National Studios of Hollywood. I mean who do we notify that you are laid up with an accident?"

"Well, I guess it won't be necessary. I am the company."

"How is that now?"

"I am National Studios of Hollywood. I am all of it."

The officer removed his foot from the chair, put his notebook away, buttoned the pocket flap, then straightened his coat by giving little tugs at the skirts. He took a deep breath, causing his leather harness to squeak audibly. "Well, now." The officer inflated his chest again, as if he liked the sound of the leather when it squeaked. "If this checks out, I guess you're all in the clear."

If this checks out. You're not out of the woods yet, Harsh thought. The cop was going to do some prying around.

The policeman had his hand on the doorknob when the door opened and the doctor came in. The doctor grinned. "How did it go, John? Get the information you needed?"

The officer patted a spot on his coat over the notebook. "I guess he told me enough to start on."

The doctor pointed to a chair. "Stick around a minute, John." The doctor took Harsh's pulse and patted him on the chest. "Nothing to keep you down, my boy." He turned to the policeman. "I have a pleasant little surprise for you, John."

"How's that, Doc?"

The doctor produced a postcard from his pocket and handed it to the officer. "Read that, John. Better read it out loud, because Mr. Harsh might like to know about it."

The officer read from the card. *"The O-Negative Blood Group Foundation. The Foundation is endowed for the purpose of aiding individuals who possess this rare blood type. Accordingly, a reward of $25.00 will be paid to any person making a direct donation of O-negative blood to another individual. An additional $25.00 will be paid to any individual instrumental in finding a donor for such a person in need of O-negative blood. The Foundation is doing this to facilitate a supply of O-negative blood. The above rewards will be paid only if immediate notice is telegraphed to the O-Negative Blood Group Foundation, 1133 Nash Street, New York, N.Y."*

The cop turned the card over. He looked puzzled. "What does this add up to?"

"It means you get twenty-five dollars, John, if you notify that outfit right away." The doctor looked pleased. "I just happened to remember that card, which came in a while back, and I dug it out of the file. John, you get twenty-five, the mechanic who donated the blood gets twenty-five. How does that strike you?"

The cop grinned. "I'll be goddamned."

The doctor waved a hand. "They got Foundations for everything these days. Some rich guy with O-negative blood probably kicked the bucket and left all his money to this Foundation, and this is the way they figure out to spend it."

Harsh had listened. It was all right with him if some bughead Foundation wanted to throw its money away, but it was a shame, he thought, to see any of it going to a cop.

THREE

The hospital was as noisy a place as Harsh had ever been in. There was continual tramping up and down the hall, talking, bottles and bedpans clanking. When finally he couldn't stand it, he yelled, "Shut the goddamn door!" Someone hurriedly closed the door, after which it was quieter, but not much. The sun was shining; if he had just felt better, it would be a good day to walk out of the hospital. The way he was now, stuck in the hospital bed, he was helpless, and anyone who wanted to do a job on him would have a free hand to do so. He was thinking of the policeman. If Harsh could get out of the hospital, he could find a private room and sack up there with no cop in his hair, stay there until he was in physical shape to cope with the situation. He could even get hold of Vera Sue if he got the notion. He fancied the idea of Vera Sue for a nurse. If a man was red-blooded, that was the stuff that would cure him.

Harsh tinkered with his left arm, feeling the cast with his fingers. It felt like a sack of concrete that had set. The arm throbbed. Could he make it out of here, he wondered, if he gave it another try? He'd better, Harsh thought. The cop was a beaver, a guy like that might hear about D. C. Roebuck being found dead in a field not all that far away and put two and two together. He picked up his left arm with his right hand and inched it toward the edge of the hospital bed. The cast weighed a ton. His hand sticking out was swollen and bluish. He clenched his teeth, worked his legs around, got them hanging off the bed. It was a high hospital bed, a long way down before his feet found the cold bare floor. He rested, panting, studying the plaster cast on his arm, noticing it was shaped so it could be carried in a sling. He pulled one of the sheets loose from the bed and tried to tear it, but his strength was not up to that, so he folded the whole sheet and knotted it in a sling that was big as a tent. His belly hurt from lying bent over backward on the bed. Okay, he thought, here it goes. He stood and took two steps and went down on the floor with a crash that shook the building and put out his lights.

Awakening, Harsh found he was back in the hospital bed. He was getting nowhere fast. He had a hazy impression he had tried to get out of the bed numerous times and each time had crashed on the floor, but that was probably all imagination. He wondered how long he had been lying there, whether it was hours or days. Then he heard a conversation outside his door. It was a nurse and the policeman, John. The cop was arguing. "Nurse, the Doc said he should be over the shock from the fall by now. He said it was okay for me to go talk to him if I wanted to."

The nurse put her head in and looked at Harsh. Unfortunately she caught him with his eyes open. "He seems to be awake. But we've had him under medication two days, so I don't know what shape he'll be in to talk."

The officer pushed past her. "I'll give it a whirl."

The cop closed the door in the nurse's face and came over to look down at Harsh. "You ever been in jail, Harsh?"

"Officer, I'm awfully sick. I can't talk to you now."

The officer ignored this. "Where were you in jail, Harsh? Come on with the answers."

"You sure are a guy who gets it wrong, Officer. I never been in anybody's pokey."

"Yeah? Then why has a detective showed up around here making inquiries about you, Harsh?"

"I don't know anything about any detective, or anybody like that."

"Neither do I, but I plan to find out. All I know, you're being investigated by somebody—the F.B.I. or a detective or someone. I ain't run into this investigator myself, as yet, but I've heard tell."

"It must be a mistake."

"Well, maybe and maybe not. I heard about it, and I'm going to look into it. I've already been looking into you, Harsh. And let me tell you, I got the stuff on you. You're one of these packs of jack-leg grafters who are traveling around our small towns skinning the people out of their money. That's what you are, and we been having trouble with your kind. Complaints, that's what. We been wanting to lay our hands on one of you skunks."

"Officer, shouldn't you be looking for the guy who sideswiped me? Isn't he the real criminal, not me?"

"Never mind that. Where is the rest of your pack of crooks?" The officer was scowling. "You birds work in gangs. Where's the rest of your outfit?"

"Officer, under the circumstances, I guess I got to give you the right answers."

"Well, what is the right answer?"

"To hell with you, you son of a bitch."

The officer started back. Anger came over his scrubbed and shaven face. "You are a dumb one, Harsh."

"I must be, if you think you can walk on me."

"We already located your gang, Harsh. One of them

anyway. Over in Edina, east of here. A young woman named Vera Sue Crosby. *Miss* Vera Sue Crosby. She said it was *Miss*, and I would say it was *Miss*. You know it is *Miss* Vera Sue Crosby, don't you, Harsh?"

"Officer, as you say, I'm pretty dumb, I don't remember."

"Maybe you would like us to speak of her as Mrs. Walter Harsh, your wife. That's how she's registered in this hotel in Edina. Mrs. Walter Harsh. But she admits her name is *Miss* Vera Sue Crosby. You see what I got on you, don't you, Harsh?"

"What you haven't got, Officer, is somebody to show you how to do your duty, to kick your fat ass into finding that hit-and-run driver who smacked into me."

"Miss Vera Sue Crosby, of Quincy, Illinois. You get it, Harsh. Quincy, Illinois. Edina, Missouri. A state line is in between those two towns, Harsh. You see now what I got? Statutory rape."

"How was that last?"

"Statutory rape. You've had it, mister."

"I may be dumb, but Mrs. Harsh never raised any kid dumb enough to have that hung on him."

"I'm talking about what the law says, Harsh. Here is a fifteen-year-old girl, and you bring her from Illinois into Missouri, which is across a state line, and you shack up with her. That is violating the Mann Act. That is statutory rape. That is up to twenty years in the Jefferson City pen."

The sides of Harsh's face felt like china saucers. The officer had not frightened him appreciably until he brought in the thing about Vera Sue being fifteen years old. Good God, she could be fifteen years old, although she had told him she was twenty-three and he had chosen to believe her. If she was fifteen and she had lied, and if they scared her into getting up in court and admitting some other things, then the cop was right, he'd had it.

The officer watched him. "What's the matter, Harsh? Don't you want to call me another dirty name? You brought a fifteen-year-old girl across the state line for immoral purposes, and that makes you the kind of a rat I like to hear call me names. That's the way I feel, only it ain't really half the way I feel."

"I'm a sick man, officer. I got an arm broken all to hell. You come back after I get some strength, I'll tell you about how I feel. I'll spit in your eye while I do it."

"I accept your invitation, Harsh, to come back. I'll bring a pair of handcuffs, too."

"You do that, while I save up spit."

"You want to tell me who this stranger is who's fishing around about you?"

"There is no such guy, and you know it."

The officer opened the door to leave. "Fellow, you are in a real mess. I hope you can see that." He went out, and Harsh lay for several minutes waiting for him to come back, but he didn't. There was a rubber sheet under Harsh, and he had perspired such a pool on it that when he turned over there was a wet sucking noise like a pig in a mud puddle.

FOUR

"Hey, Doc."

"Yes, Harsh."

"You gotta fix it so I can use a phone."

"You're in no shape to do any telephoning, Harsh."

"Listen, I got to hit the telephone, Doc. It's urgent."
He was talking around a thermometer the doctor had
stuck in his mouth.

The doctor came over and took out the thermometer,
put on his glasses, and threw his head back to see through
the bifocals. Then he took Harsh's pulse.

"The cop sort of upset you, eh?"

"Sort of."

"He's a pretty nice guy, really."

"Yeah, it was easy to see what a nice guy he is. What
about me and the telephone?"

"Well I tell you what, you rest a few hours, get some
sleep. Then we may fix you up with a telephone call."

"Doc, it can't wait."

"Well, it can try."

Walter Harsh lay on the hospital bed and thought about
the photography business. The way it was, anyone who
could get together a dollar ninety-eight could be a photographer, for that would buy a cheap box with a piece of
windowglass for a lens and a roll of low-cost film. That
put anyone in business, the snapshot business, and that
was the trouble, since that was all the value the public

put on it. The twelve-jumbo-size-prints-for-thirty-five-cents roll film finishing business was another problem, a picture for less than a nickel. That was the price tag John Q. Public liked to put on a picture, and anything above that, they called it robbery. That made it a difficult business.

Harsh was a good portrait photographer, he was sure of that. He had started out very young with a cheap snap box when he was a kid on the farm, securing his camera for the labels off five sacks of hog supplement and a dollar. He sold muskrat pelts to buy a roll of film, sold more muskrat hides and a mink he was lucky enough to trap and bought some D76 and hypo and contact paper. Later when the army got him, he talked his way into a photo section, where he learned a lot. He used the G.I. Bill of Rights to go to a photographer's school in Kansas City and another portrait school in New York. By then he was a good portrait man. He was no Bannerman, no Kirsh, but he was an above average portrait man.

He had thought that would be enough, but it wasn't. He soon decided there were only two ways up as a photographer, and both ways required a gimmick. The best gimmick, which was out of his reach, was a plushy downtown studio with chrome-edged showcases and plenty of gold-toned sepia samples and a blond office girl and a reputation for high prices and being twenty years in the business. The other way up was to go out and knuckle doors. That had its drawbacks, since just about every town had an ordinance against door knocking and an out-of-towner needed a gimmick to get around this. Harsh knew he was right about one thing, the ordinances were barriers the local sit-on-his-bottom photo-

grapher had talked the city fathers into passing to protect his laziness. So Harsh felt no remorse about the
gimmick he was using.

Harsh's gimmick was tailored for small towns. He
would send a woman with a nice-sounding voice into the
small town a few days in advance to rent desk space and a
telephone and buy some spot announcements over the
local radio station. Then the woman would sit down at
the telephone in the rented desk space and turn to A in
the directory and call every subscriber through to Z.
"Good morning, Mrs. Aarons. This is Miss Crosby, with
National Studios of Hollywood. Mrs. Aarons, you have
heard our program on the radio, no doubt. If you can
answer today's quiz question, you will receive an absolutely wonderful big free prize of three size eight-by-ten
portrait photographs of yourself and any other two mem-
bers of your family. If you heard our sponsored program
today, you will receive an extra listener's prize."

The quiz question that won the prize was a real toughie:
"Mrs. Aarons, who succeeded Franklin D. Roosevelt as
President of the United States? Now take your time and
think." The person being called on the telephone always
won the wonderful big free prize, because Harsh had to
get into their homes to shoot the negatives and come
back and push the prints. It was legitimate. The mark got
the three free pictures, and unless he could say no faster
than a squirrel chatters, he would find twenty or thirty
dollars worth of additional prints crammed down his
throat. Harsh would snap a lot of shots of the kids with
their toys and he had a way of putting all the prints
together in an accordion-pleat folder that the parents
went for. When he flipped all those shots of the kid

out on the living-room rug, mom's eyes would pop.
The telephone quiz gimmick got them around the anti-
door-knocker law, the radio gave a cloak of respectability
and substance, and National Studios of Hollywood, that
sounded like something too.

Vera Sue Crosby was Harsh's advance girl. Vera Sue
went into the small towns and rented the desk space and
the telephone and did the calling. Vera Sue was a real
gem in a boiler room. She had a voice like the Mona Lisa
over the telephone, a nun-pure voice that sounded naive
and honest. The voice certainly didn't sound like Vera
Sue, as full of sex as a thirty-dollar call house.

There was sunshine in the room when the doctor came in
and thrust the thermometer in Harsh's mouth, which was
less embarrassing than having it stuck in his bottom the
way the nurses had been doing. Harsh watched the
doctor stand there counting pulse with one eye narrowed
at his wristwatch while he waited for the thermometer to
stabilize.

"Well, Harsh, I guess you are up to it. If you still want,
you can use the telephone."

The doctor brought a telephone with a long cord and
plugged it into an outlet in the wall and put the instrument on the bed. Harsh seized it, the hospital operator
came on the wire, and he placed a person-to-person call
to Mrs. Walter Harsh in Edina, Missouri. When the doctor
heard that, he looked surprised. "I didn't understand you
were married, Harsh."

Better get the old pill-snapper out of the room, Harsh
thought. "Look, Doc, this is kind of personal. Do you
mind?"

"Harsh, if you're married we should have notified—"

"Doc, you stick to your pills and your thermometer, and leave the women to me, then we would both know what we were doing."

The doctor went out reluctantly. An old guy like him, wanting to eavesdrop, when he should be sitting on a creek bank waiting for a catfish to grab a worm, Harsh reflected.

"Vera Sue?"

"Walter!"

"I wasn't sure my call would catch you, after all this time."

"Walter, honey, pep it up, will you? I mean, whatever you got to say, get it said."

"Well, for crying out loud, aren't you the interested one! Haven't you wondered where I was? Listen, I had an accident, and I'm in the hospital."

"I know where you are. Walter, the bus is about due, and the man said it was always on time."

"Where are you catching a bus to?"

"To see you, what do you think? I already got my ticket, Walter, so don't talk all day."

"Good for you, baby. Jesus, I'm glad you used your head so quick. I didn't know you had it in you. But listen, here's what you do first. I need you to stop off in Illinois. The minute you get back to Illinois, the very minute you get in Illinois, dig up your birth certificate. Birth certificate. You got that?"

"Walter, I can't."

"You can't?" He lowered his voice. "You don't mean you really are fifteen years old? Goddamn you if you lied to me—"

"Don't you goddamn me, Walter, I am twenty-three and you know it."

"All right, as soon as you hit Illinois, you dig up a birth certificate to prove it. Otherwise I'm on the hook. If you don't dig up a birth certificate, they're going to soak me with the Mann Act and statutory rape and God only knows what. They claim you're fifteen years old. I don't know where they got that fifteen stuff. Did you tell them anything like that?"

Vera Sue burst into laughter. Her laughter was a wonderful sound like a nightingale chorusing out in the moonlight. "I was only kidding the cop. He was such a square."

"You picked a great lie to tell him."

"It was just a joke."

"It was some joke. He came in here and scared the bejesus out of me with that fifteen story. Is that how you found I was knocked out in the hospital? Did the cop tell you?"

"Yes. But did you know there's someone else checking on you too?"

"Who?"

"A private cop. From Kansas City, I think. Anyway he's going around asking all kinds of questions and showing your picture."

"There really is such a guy? I thought the cop was stringing me."

"Well, you were wrong, Walter. This fellow talked to me quite a while, wanting to know different things about you and showing me this picture he had of you. Listen, Walter, when did you have the scar taken off your face?"

"Scar taken off my face? I never had a scar on my face."

"I saw it."

"What are you talking about? Where?"

"On your left cheek, high up. A fair-sized scar."

"That proves they're looking for somebody else, not me. I never had such a scar, never in my life."

"But Walter, it looked just like you, I recognized you right off. The only difference was the scar. And it described you, down to the last detail, even your blood type, O-negative."

"Goddamn it, you fell for something, some kind of racket. You know why I'm sure? Because nobody knew I had O-negative blood, not even me, until I lit in this hospital."

"Well, this guy knew it. Anyway, I'm coming over there. If you think I am going to pay no attention to five thousand dollars floating around, you're crazy. I got my bus ticket, and if you shut up, I may catch my bus."

"Wait a minute, what's this about five thousand dollars?"

"This private peeper from Kansas City told me there was five thousand dollars in it if you turned out to be 'completely acceptable,' whatever that means. I asked him, but he either didn't know or put on the clam. Anyway, I'm coming over to see if I can get a piece of that five thousand for baby."

"You must have got real chummy with this fellow from Kansas City."

"Oh, we had a couple of short beers. I found out that was enough to make him windy."

"Listen, Vera Sue, you go to Illinois and get that birth certificate."

"Nothing doing. I'll be sitting on the edge of your bed in a couple of hours."

He thought they would come and take the telephone away as soon as he hung up, but no one came. It seemed like time was turning into forever as he lay there with the stuff they had been shooting into him beginning to wear off so that his arm felt like a balloon full of pain. His head seemed to be trying to split itself. He wished he was out of the hospital. He wondered how it would go if he would roll out of the bed and let himself down on the floor real easy and crawl on the floor into the hall and out of the place. It wouldn't work, of course, but a man could wish.

He lay back, breathing heavily, his head feeling as though it was rolling over and over down a hill. A private detective from Kansas City, how did you figure that one? If D. C. Roebuck had had insurance, then the man might be an insurance company investigator engaged in getting the goods on him. The idea worried him. An insurance detective could be worse than the police. A damn insurance company, he thought, didn't care how much it spent as long as it was trying to get out of paying a claim.

Sweat had come out on him while he was talking on the telephone to Vera Sue and since, and he was wet with it. He was in bad shape. Being so helpless brought tears of rage to his eyes. Here he was like a mouse with its tail caught in the trap, he reflected, and all the cats walking around smacking lips. One cat, two cats, three cats. The city policeman, the Kansas City sherlock, and now Vera Sue, trying to cut herself in on a reward at his expense…

He did not remember going to sleep, but he awakened when the doctor came in. He felt very weak and shaky.

"Doc, you sure stayed away long enough."

"I was invited to leave, remember?"

"Ah, Doc, don't be an old woman. You know, I don't feel so hot."

"What's the matter? The arm hurt?"

"The arm, the head, all over. I feel like one big sore ball, Doc, you want to know the truth."

The thermometer went into his mouth again, feeling like an icicle, while the doctor counted his pulse. "You have some temperature. What happened with that telephone call to upset you this way?"

"Nothing, Doc, that I know of."

They brought in a transparent canopy and set it up on the bed with him inside, then wheeled in a cylinder that had gauges on it and a tube running under the canopy. They hooked up the thing, and stood watching the gauges while the tube hissed close to his nose. "Doc, what is this thing?"

"An oxygen tent."

"That's what they put on guys who are dying, ain't it? Take it away. I'm afraid of the thing."

"We probably won't be that lucky with you."

The morning sun was splintering into his eyes. The way the sunlight was hitting the oxygen tent canopy he could see very little in the room. Finally he realized someone was sitting by the bed. A nurse, he thought, sitting there like an albino crow waiting for him to die. "Nurse, I got to piss."

There was a giggle. The corner of the oxygen tent was

lifted and Vera Sue looked in at him. "Hello, Walter."

She kissed him. He kissed her back. Her mouth was warm and moist, tasting of spearmint.

"Jesus, honey, what I said there a minute ago. I thought you were the nurse."

"It was kind of funny, Walter."

"She's an old crow, always sticking her cold thermometer in my ass."

"Walter, I been sitting here a long time. They told me not to wake you—they said I could sit in here, but I should let you sleep. I told them a lie. I said I was your wife."

"I wondered how you got in."

"Walter…I couldn't go to Illinois. I couldn't make myself do it. You know something, after I talked to you on the telephone, I missed my bus sitting there trying to make myself go to Illinois like you wanted, but I just couldn't."

"Baby, I knew you wouldn't, so you can stop kidding around."

She kissed him and held him close. Her moist mouth moved all over his. "I'm glad you're not mad. Walter, I wish I could get in bed with you right now."

"That would be something. I bet this oxygen stuff would go flying all over, and somebody would come in to see what was wrecking the joint."

"I wouldn't give a damn if they did."

A nurse came in with two glasses of orange juice, one for him and one for Mrs. Harsh, she said. The nurse was a different one, a large plain woman.

"Walter, is she the nurse you were talking about?"

"No, but she gives you an idea." He lay back holding

his orange juice. "Well, I'm glad you're here. You got no idea what it is to be nailed down like this. Now, what was this about a detective from Kansas City asking about me?"

"Hasn't he been around to see you yet?"

"I haven't seen him, but I don't know if he was here or not. I made the Doc think I was too sick to be bothered."

"That's funny. I got the idea he was finding out all about you, getting ready to offer you a proposition. I don't really understand what he's up to, Walter. He didn't say you were accused of anything. He just said there was five thousand in it for him if you turned out to be acceptable and satisfactory, and he would appreciate anything I could tell him about you. He didn't seem to be after any specific information, just general stuff. Walter, what is he up to?"

"I sure would like to know myself."

"You sure got to help me figure a way to get my mitts on that five thousand."

"Our mitts, you mean, don't you?"

"What? Oh, sure, that's what I mean."

"Vera Sue, you be careful. You let me know before you make any moves. You let me supply the brains around here."

"Well, how about me working some more on Kansas City as our first move?"

"All right with me. But watch out for that local city cop, John Something-or-other. He's no pushover. How are you going to get in touch with this Kansas City dude?"

"I'm going to call him and invite him to have breakfast with me. He left me his hotel address here."

"Say, I would like to have a look at that picture the guy

is showing around, the one that looks like me except for the scar on the face. Can you swing that?"

"I bet I can, Walter."

He would bet she would too.

At noon they gave him a lamb chop and some mashed potatoes and peas and a cigarette and a newspaper. The policeman had not come back. The doctor had not come back. And Vera Sue had not come back. He had turned into a forgotten man, he decided, and it was all right with him. He was nervous. His mind was jumpy. He thought of his mind as acting like a bird with its legs chopped off so it couldn't come to roost on anything.

He lay there with his fists clenched and his eyes closed, and one of the things he could not keep out of his mind was the way D. C. Roebuck's car had gone over and over in the field, in one of the flips landing (he was now able to remember) on D. C. Roebuck himself.

Suddenly he remembered the newspaper they had brought him with his lunch. What was wrong with him? A thing as important as the newspaper, and he had hardly noticed it. Where was the paper anyway, on the floor, or where? He saw the paper on the floor, and when he leaned off the bed for it, the blood ran to his head and made him dizzy, and he almost fell off the bed before he clutched the newspaper.

The story from Carrollton, Missouri, was a small item on an inside page. It said the body of D. C. Roebuck, Kansas City photographic supply salesman, had been found with his demolished automobile in a field near Carrollton Friday and had been taken to his home in

Kansas City for burial. That was all. Nothing there to hook him up with Roebuck's death, he reflected, though that did not necessarily mean a thing. He imagined the police, and even more so an insurance company, worked undercover until they had all the evidence they wanted, then bang, they let you have it.

The next thing was the jury. The idea of a court trial worried him, but if he had to have one, he hoped the jury would be made up of farmers, so he could have his lawyer bring out that he grew up on a farm. Thinking about his early days on the farm made him feel maudlin. It was a good life, that farm, and he wished he had stuck with it. He would have, too, only a man needed a million dollars and a million acres to make a go on the farm; it was just impossible for a young man to save enough to start farming. It was equally hopeless the way his own parents had tried to make it, which was by share-farming. It was all the same hind tit and impossible to suck more than a bare existence out of it. But one thing he could say for the farm, it was man against nature, and not man against man the way it was in the city. In the city it was every man for himself: talk sweet and polite, act like a shark. He had to laugh at the memory of how he came off the farm a green one, and he had taken it in the neck too, until he got unsquared. Since then, he had handed them back a few licks himself.

Better have the lawyer soft pedal that to the jury, he thought, the jury might not understand quite how it was, on the bum, hitchhiking, pearl-diving for handouts, even panhandling. He had been in the pokey three or four times; he had not told the policeman the truth about that.

What the hell, he thought, it was none of the town law's business.

He wondered if the cop had shared that twenty-five bucks around. He would bet not. The town cop was just like anybody else, give them a whiff of easy money, put the golden odor in their nose, and they went haywire. Free money was the worst. Take the big free prize National Studios of Hollywood offered the marks over the telephone, it was not much, just three portraits that cost twenty-five cents apiece to turn out. But it was free, something for nothing, and common sense went flapping out of the window. Like Vera Sue, he thought, and that five thousand dollars she was chasing with her tongue hanging out. All she had to go on, some guy she had barely met had said somebody was paying him five thousand dollars for something that didn't make sense. And Vera Sue was hard at it, trying to grab the five thousand as if it was right there in front of her. The smell of money had her wild.

But maybe the worst was, he could smell it a little himself.

Early in the afternoon the nurse came in. "Mr. Harsh, a letter for you."

"For me? Who would be writing me?"

It was a large plain envelope with his name on it, a special delivery stamp, and the name of the hospital. Inside was a photograph. Nothing else. Harsh had a look at the photograph. He put it under his pillow in a hurry.

"Nurse."

"Yes."

"If you will close the door when you go out, I guess I will have me a nap."

The nurse did not take the hint right away, but fussed around a while longer with the sheets, put out a fresh glass of water with the bent glass straw in it, and put the bedpan where he could reach it. Finally she left, closing the door.

Harsh got the picture out and had a long look at it. The thing was as close a likeness to him as he could imagine, except for the scar, which began at the left eye corner and ran down and forward, a scar about three inches long.

FIVE

He was smearing scrambled egg on toast and taking slow bites when Vera Sue came in the next morning. It was ten o'clock. Vera Sue wore a grey sweater, tight-fitting, a shiny wide black belt, and a charcoal skirt with enough material in it for several skirts. She had a pert and jouncy new charcoal hat with a feather. She came to him and began kissing him. He held her and kissed back. Presently an embarrassed smile came to the nurse's face, and she left the room.

"Walter, did you get my letter?"

He feigned surprise. "What letter was that?"

"You didn't get it? A special delivery I sent you?"

"Never heard of it."

Vera Sue slapped her forehead with her palm. "Oh, Jesus Christ, Walter, something went wrong."

"Well, somebody did send me a picture of myself, or my almost-self."

She leaned over and damn near bit the end off his nose. "There! That will teach you to joke."

"Sure I got your letter and I must say it convinced me I was wrong about there not being any picture. Ouch! Goddamn, you could ruin the end of a man's nose that way."

"Walter, you scared me. I thought that cop had got wise or something and headed it off."

"How did you get the picture?"

"Off of Kansas City. I picked his pocket."

"That's okay, as long as his pants weren't hanging on the bedpost when the pocket got picked."

"Walter, you know me better than that." She slapped her forehead with her hand again. "Walter! For God's sake, your face!"

"Huh?"

"What did you do to your face?"

"This? Oh, that's an experiment." What he had done was take a teaspoon, the one out of the medicine glass on the table by the bed, and place the edge of the handle across his cheek about where the picture showed the scar to be. Then he had lain on the spoon handle. He had been lying on the spoon handle nearly an hour, and it had made a groove in his face. "Let me have the mirror out of your purse, so I can check on the results."

"Walter, why did you do that?"

"You took your time noticing it. Let's see the mirror."

She fished in her purse, found the mirror, and he held it in front of his face, moving his head from side to side to view the results of his experiment. There was a deep crease on his cheek. It looked somewhat like a scar. He was stunned at the resemblance he now bore to the picture.

"I wish you hadn't fooled with your face, Walter."

"This really makes me the double for the guy in the picture, though, don't it? That's what I wanted to find out."

Vera Sue began to walk around the room. "I'm not so sure. You may have fouled things up."

"How is that?"

"A man's here."

"Who? Your guy from Kansas City?"

"No, a man from New York. A new man. Mr. Brother, he said his name is."

"Mr. Brother? I don't know anybody by that name."

"Well, he's here now."

"How in the name of creeping Jesus did he happen to show up, and what does he want?"

"That John What's-his-name, the city policeman, sent him a telegram."

"Oh, that. The O-Negative Blood Foundation thing. Twenty-five bucks reward for everybody connected with getting that blood except the guy who needed it, which is me. The cop was supposed to telegraph to get the reward. If you ask me, it's as cockeyed as the rest of this. You say this Mr. Brother is here? Here at the hospital?"

Vera Sue nodded quickly. "He's in the waiting room now."

"Right outside?"

"Yes."

"Oh what a stupid trick, bringing him here now."

Vera Sue's face became sullen. "Don't call me stupid."

Harsh was angry that she hadn't consulted him. If she were standing a little closer, he thought, he would give her one with his fist, smack her across the room. He would teach her to talk over a move with him before she made it. Then he felt shaky inside, realizing he was helpless here in bed, and if Vera Sue walked out on him, he would really be up the creek.

"Vera Sue, I'm sorry. I shouldn't have called you dumb. I guess I said it because I'm sick."

She took the mirror away from him and put it in her purse. "You're a no good son of a bitch, did you know that?"

"Yes, I'm no good, and I'm sorry and I love you."

"The hell with you, Walter." She adjusted her new hat. "I'm going to bring in Mr. Brother."

Just wait until he got up and around, he thought, and he would show her a couple of things.

Brother was a soft-looking man in an extremely neat brown suit. He had a straight slender nose with no flare at the nostrils, a nose like a hatchet blade. He had thick lips, oversize brown eyes. His skin was tanned a trifle lighter shade of brown than his suit, which was a ripe tobacco leaf. He carried a leather briefcase, the folder type without a handle that closes with a zipper. He kept the case under his right arm.

"Mr. Harsh?" He had a pronounced accent which Harsh identified at once as Spanish.

"That's me."

The man stepped to the bedside and took a close look at him. The effect on him was violent. His hands tightened convulsively on the briefcase. Harsh got the impression the man wanted to leap upon him and strike him, that the man hated him utterly and irrationally at first sight.

"Mister, the scar ain't real, if that's what startled you."

"El hermano, por Dios!" The man's eyes protruded. They were shiny and brown like the eyes of a choked dog.

Presently the man stepped back and hauled out a tan silk handkerchief of unusual size. By the time he had blotted his hands, lips and forehead, he had regained some control. He turned to Vera Sue. "Will you step outside, Miss, in order that Mr. Harsh and I may be alone?"

Vera Sue looked so disappointed that Harsh wanted to laugh. She had been going around doing as she damn

pleased, he thought, and missing out on this talk was
going to brown her off good. Vera Sue finally went out,
but left the door open.

Brother closed the door, came back to the bed, seized
the sheet and gave it a jerk, exposing Harsh in the alto-
gether. "Hey! What's the idea, Mister?"

"Turn over."

"Mister, just who do you think you are, coming in here
and yanking the covers off me and ordering me ass up
and belly down? Who the hell do you think you are?"
When he got that much said, Harsh wished he had kept
still. It was the look that came into the man's eyes. It
made the hair on the back of Harsh's neck turn cold, as if
a frosty-footed mouse had walked across his spine. Harsh
turned over on the bed as directed. The way he was lying
then, he could not see the man's face, but the effect of the
stare stayed with him. Jesus, was the guy nuts? "Mister, I
got this bum arm and lying this way it don't feel too hot.
How about turning back the way I was?"

After an uncomfortable few moments longer, Harsh
felt the sheet come back down over him. He rotated onto
his back once more.

"The young lady indicated she would tell you who I
am," Mr. Brother said.

"She said a man named Mr. Brother was here to see
me. She didn't say anybody would come in here jerking
the covers off me."

"Who told you to put that mark on the side of your
face?"

"Nobody. I just laid the wrong way, something under
my face."

"You are lying to me, Mr. Harsh." There was a carefulness about the way he formed his words that indicated he did his thinking in another language—either that, or that he was straining to hold back a monumental temper.

"Fine. I saw a photograph of a face looked something like mine, only it had a scar. I wanted to see how such a scar would look on me, so I laid down on the spoon handle. And you happened to show up before the marks went away."

The man didn't respond—it was as if he hadn't heard. Everything Harsh said or did seemed to be beneath contempt to him. He whipped out a sheet of blank paper, folded it precisely, uncapped a fountain pen.

"Mr. Harsh, how would you like to earn twenty-five dollars? I will pay you five dollars each for five names. The five names are to be of people who have known you within the last few years."

"How is that? You mean you want references of some sort—but you want to *buy* them from me?"

The man looked at Harsh as if he was considering spitting on him. "I wouldn't think a man like you does much without being bought."

"Look, goddamn you, I can be run over just about so far."

The man's face became calm, but his eyes glittered. "Mr. Harsh, the only way I will deal with you is to buy you. I do not care to work with you on any other basis. I buy you or nothing. You are a cheap man, so buying you will not be expensive. Get it straight—I buy you, or I have nothing to do with you."

Harsh lifted himself on his good elbow. "Look, I don't

know why you should be such a crock, but if you want references, I'll give them to you for nothing. I won't sell them, though. I got some pride too."

Harsh was amazed when the man capped the fountain pen, put it away, tucked the blank paper in his pocket, and strode purposefully to the door. He was going to leave, the crazy fool, twenty-five dollars was going to walk out the door.

"Hey, Mister! If you insist, I'll take your money."

Again the man seemed not to hear, and walked out the door, leaving Harsh watching the door and waiting, hardly believing the fellow was gone. Harsh watched the door for some time. His arm, which had been giving only mild pain, now started hurting in earnest. It felt as if a cat was crouched on it, eating away. No one came through the door, not Brother, not Vera Sue, not the policeman, not even a doctor or a nurse.

What should he make of this Brother anyway, he wondered.

Several hours later when Vera Sue did appear, he saw she had been up to something. She was as warm and contented as a baby who had found a full breast, and she was wearing a new dress with the new hat. "Oh, Walter, he is just slightly terrific, isn't he?"

Harsh scowled at her. He did not know who she was talking about, but he would bet it was somebody who wore pants with well-filled pockets. "Where have you been all day?"

"Don't be sore. Someone had to show Mr. Brother around, after he came all the way out here to Missouri from the east just to look you over. And you should see

what he came in. Walter, you should see it! He has a big
private airplane all his very own."

"Is Brother still around here?" Harsh lifted up on the
bed. "The way he took out of here as if he'd been turpen-
tined, I figured school was out. Did he leave for good?"

"And what an airplane, Walter. Instead of just seats for
passengers, private cabins and a private office and a private television set. Inside, it's all lined with velvet that's a
kind of bedroom purple and the two fellas flying the
thing for him wear liveries the same purple color."

Harsh was speechless with rage.

Vera Sue lifted on tiptoes and did a turn in front of
him. "Walter, notice anything new has been added?"

"Goddamn it!" His voice shook with fury. "I asked you,
is the guy still in town?"

"Yes. Didn't you notice my new dress?"

"The hell with the new dress."

"Walter, I wish you wouldn't be nasty. I like to hear
you say nice things about my clothes, and not growl at me
like a bear."

He wanted to grab hold of her, shake some sense into
her—but he forced himself to grin weakly instead. "Sure,
honey, I know. It's just that I lie here not knowing what's
going on and it makes me blow my top."

"Well, it isn't very nice."

Walter bit back a curse. "I'm nuts about you, honey,
you know that."

"You're awfully sweet when you want to be, Walter. I
wish you would want to be all the time."

"Kiss me, honey."

She kissed him and he discovered her mouth tasted of
eight-dollar-a-bottle Benedictine. So she had gotten her

hands on more than just what it took to buy the new dress and the new hat. The Benedictine was a giveaway, because on special occasions she would buy a bottle and carry it around in her purse and nip at it. He suspected that someone had once told her Benedictine was the *liqueur* of quality folks, but had neglected to tell her it was supposed to be sipped out of thimble-sized glasses after dinner. Anyway, she had gotten hold of some money, and he had a good idea where.

"Vera Sue, I hope you didn't go making any deals with this Brother guy. We can't until we know more than we know now."

"How do you mean, Walter?"

"He gave you some dough, right?"

She stroked her hair with her hand, and the innocent expression on her face told him she was trying to think up a lie.

"Look, Vera Sue, it's all right with me for you to latch on to his money. I got no kicks, I want you to have dough, only you should talk it over with me first."

"I was almost broke, Walter, and you were acting snotty."

He controlled his fury with difficulty. "Well, like I say, I got no kicks. But baby, the only thing is, you and me are in this together, and we got to keep our eyes open. I know how to handle guys like Brother, so you better let me handle him. I'll give you a sample of how I would handle him. He wanted me to give him some references, see, but he's not going to get any names from me for nothing. I'm going to make him pay me five dollars a name. If he wants five names, it will cost him twenty-five bucks."

Vera Sue's expression became odd. "How much for each name, Walter?"

"Five dollars. He pays five bucks, or he won't get a single name."

Vera Sue's mouth started twitching, and suddenly a shriek of laughter escaped her. She laughed so hard that she had to lean on the bed for support.

Harsh glared. "What's killing you now?"

"Walter, you sure are some whiz-bang businessman."

"Huh?"

She picked up a corner of the bed sheet and wiped the tears of mirth out of her eyes. "So, you can get five dollars a name. Five dollars." She blew her nose in the sheet.

"Yeah, at least that much."

"I got one hundred dollars, Walter. That's what I got apiece for five names. Five hundred dollars. You say you can get five a name, but I got one hundred. What do you say to that?"

Harsh tried to sit up but his arm shot pain through his body and he lay back gasping. "You got five hundred?" What was there for him to say? He could not remember when any news had made him feel so sick and defeated. He swallowed some of his own saliva, and it tasted like gall. "Hand over my share."

"What?"

"Hand over my share of what you got, baby. My half."

She withdrew a step. "Your share is half of twenty-five bucks, Walter, if you got any share coming."

"Don't start pulling stuff like that, Vera Sue."

"Listen, lover boy, I talk to dumb clucks any way I want, and you're a dumb cluck, and also a cheap cluck. You're a five-dollar cluck, that's what you are."

He struggled to a sitting position on the bed, ignoring the pain from his arm. "You watch out, or I'll bat you one."

She laughed nastily and buttoned the new coat over her new dress. "If that's the way you feel, you can go to hell."

She left the hospital room, not bothering to close the door. He fell back on the bed, causing his arm to hurt violently, and looked silently at the ceiling. Presently, when the nurse put her head in the door and looked at him and saw the expression on his face, she gasped and came in and thrust the thermometer in his mouth and took his pulse. She carried the thermometer to the window to examine it and shook her head, murmuring that if visitors excited him so much, he would just have to stop having them. Harsh bellowed at her, "Jesus God, get out of here and leave me alone!" This made the nurse angry, and instead of leaving the room, she forced him to take a drink of water, jamming the glass against his teeth hard enough that it grated. He swallowed some water. She placed the glass on the table and snatched an object off a chair. "Who left this here?"

Harsh looked and saw that she had picked up Brother's briefcase. He had not noticed Brother had left it behind.

"They left it here for me to look at." He turned his face away from the nurse so she would not see he was lying. "Why don't you get out of here?"

The nurse shrugged, put the briefcase back on the chair, and left.

Harsh did not move a muscle for a while, thinking she might come back. He was furious about the five hundred dollar thing. He had as much right to the money as anybody, but getting it away from the greedy bitch was another thing. He found it incomprehensible that Brother should pay five hundred dollars for five names which

Harsh had offered to give the man for nothing. It proved one thing, he decided, it proved Brother was no insurance company detective. No insurance company would hire a man who threw their money around in such a crazy way.

He became convinced the nurse was not coming back, and he turned crosswise on the bed, stretching out his serviceable arm for Brother's briefcase. He was able to reach it and drag it onto the bed. It was not locked. He gripped the zipper tab with his fingers and pulled it open. He looked inside.

What is this thing? he thought. He lifted out a device with a leatherette covering. It was about the size of a cigar box for twenty-five cigars. On the outside were two knobs and a red light. When he accidentally tapped the device while handling it, he noticed the light glow.

He got it. The device was a battery-driven wire recorder. Since the light was glowing, it obviously was operating. There was nothing else in the briefcase.

More frosting on the cake, he thought.

He considered smashing the recorder against the floor or at least pulling the wire off the uptake spool and ruining it, crumpling it into a little metal wad—but in the end he just put the device back and returned the briefcase to the chair.

Let the bastard hear what he wanted to hear. Maybe it would mean getting to the bottom of things that much faster.

SIX

If Harsh retained any doubts about Brother being an
oddball, they were removed when Brother paid a second
visit. Harsh was lying with his eyes closed trying to doze.
Four or five hours had gone by and he had more or less
calmed down. He knew he needed rest. When he heard
the door open, he supposed the nurse was back, and he
kept his eyes shut until he heard the newcomer pick up
the briefcase and heard the zipper rasp as it opened.
Harsh lifted his head.

Brother was removing the little wire recorder from
the case, and looking at Harsh with an expression of contempt. Without speaking he placed the recorder on the
bed and turned one of its knobs. The recorder whirred as
it rewound. Brother adjusted the knobs again. The recorder began to talk, playing back what Brother and
Harsh had said on their first meeting. Then came what
Vera Sue and Harsh had said to each other. The device
evidently had a triggering mechanism so that it only
recorded when there was sound being made in range of
the microphone.

Brother shut it off. His lips twitched with amusement.
"The young lady made a fool of you."

Harsh had decided he was not going to let the man get
his goat. "Did she?"

"She showed you up."

"Well, if you say so."

"Harsh, I can tell you something that may make you

feel better. She did not have any idea of asking five hundred dollars for those names. Or asking anything. I merely made her the offer and she grabbed it."

Harsh gave this some thought. "Can you prove Vera Sue didn't make a fool out of both of us?"

"How is that?"

"You paid her five hundred dollars for something worth nothing. What does that make you? I may have been a dope, but I didn't pay out five hundred for the privilege."

Brother shook his head. "You miss the point."

"I guess I miss it, all right. What is the point?"

"Everything has to be done my way."

"That is the point?"

"Exactly. Everything has to be done my way. Remember that. When I ordered you to give me five references in return for twenty-five dollars and you refused, I paid the young woman five hundred dollars for the same information. I was teaching you a lesson. I hope you got it."

Harsh reached out a hand and his fingers felt on the table for cigarettes. Dumb bastard, Harsh thought. He pulled a cigarette out of the pack and put it between his lips. I'll be goddamned if I ever heard the like of this.

"Mr. Brother, you gave me something to think about, I admit that."

"When I give an order, it must be obeyed without question or haggling. That is what I am trying to establish. Do you understand?"

"I don't know how you could say it any plainer, Mr. Brother."

"But do you comprehend?"

"Sure."

"I doubt it, Harsh." Brother's eyes were contemptuous.

"I do not think you are very good at comprehension."

"If you want to think so, okay. You could be wrong, though."

"No, Harsh. I have had you investigated thoroughly."

Harsh lifted his hand, removed the cigarette from his lips, and looked at it. He did not want the man to see his expression. "I heard there was a private detective from Kansas City snooping around. Was he your boy?"

"One of them. One of about twenty."

"I don't know what you thought that would get you." Harsh rolled the cigarette slowly in his fingers.

Brother smiled with dislike. "It got *you* something, Harsh."

"It did? How is that?"

"It enabled me to arrange to protect you from the police in the matter of D. C. Roebuck." The man's teeth were small white chisel edges under his lifted lip. "Providing you cooperate, of course."

Harsh closed his eyes. For a moment he thought he was going to faint. His hand holding the cigarette lay limp on his chest.

"Harsh, I am going to talk steadily for several minutes. Making explanations. Do not interrupt."

Harsh's mouth was becoming very dry. He merely nodded his head.

"Harsh, I have been searching for a man to fit a certain exact description. The man must look exactly like the picture you have seen. He must have O-negative blood. The man must be of near criminal character, and he must be for sale. To find such a man I set up a so-called foundation and offered a reward, twenty-five dollars, for each O-negative blood donor, and I have expended many thousands of dollars fruitlessly on the device. Finally a local policeman notified me of someone who had needed such a donor here. It was you. I had a firm of private detectives from Kansas City investigate you at once, as I have had every possible candidate investigated in the past. The detectives found you had crowded D. C. Roebuck off the road and he was killed. They found a man in a service station in Carrollton, Missouri, who saw Mr. Roebuck drive away in pursuit of you. I have had them pay the service station man in Carrollton a sum of money to be silent. My detectives also found that locally the police wished to charge you with statutory rape, and I have stopped that by obtaining a birth certificate showing Miss Crosby is over twenty-one years of age. I have sold your car, and you will receive the price of a new one. I have paid your hospital bill here. The private detectives have checked your references, and I find you are a borderline crook. I have paid off the detectives, and they are gone. In other words, you are satisfactory, Harsh. I find you acceptable. Therefore only one thing remains to be settled."

Harsh slowly put the cigarette between his lips. He felt for the book of matches on the bedside table, bent a match back to light it one-handed, and held the flame to the end of the cigarette. He noticed his hand was unsteady. He took one puff, and after that the cigarette hung on his lip with the tip smoldering.

"Mister, you kind of took the wind out of my sails."

"You have questions, Harsh?" A sneer curled his lip.

"Yeah, I got a bushel of questions, Mister. You say you bought the service station guy in Carrollton, but will he stay—"

"I will answer no questions whatever, Harsh. You have been told the essential facts. That is sufficient."

Harsh frowned at the thin curl of blue smoke coming off the end of the cigarette. "You're kind of a puzzle to me, Mister."

"Are you for sale, Harsh?"

"Eh?"

"Are you for sale. You heard me."

Harsh took the cigarette away to moisten his lips with his tongue. "I admit taking Roebuck off my neck is worth something. But will it stick? I got to know more about—"

"I am talking about selling yourself for dollars, Harsh."

"Oh. Well, you hadn't mentioned money, only Roebuck, and I thought you meant one favor in exchange for another."

"I will never need a favor from a man of your caliber, Harsh."

"Well, if you say so. But a man never knows."

"I asked you if you were for sale, you fool." The man looked at Harsh with eyes as cold and moist as those of a dead cow.

"I guess the answer is yes."

"Good. It is settled." Brother began buttoning his topcoat preparatory to leaving. "This is as far as our discussion need go."

"Wait a minute." Harsh stubbed out the cigarette. "Nobody said how much money we're discussing."

"I already know your price tag, Harsh." Brother drew a package of money from his pocket and tossed it on the bed. "That is the full amount we are discussing. There will be no more. Count it. It is not yours until your job is done. I will be back later."

The sheaf of currency was held by a rubber band. It had come to rest exactly in the middle of Harsh's stomach. He could see it by looking down his nose. He did not touch it.

"Harsh."

"Yes?"

"You are to be removed from this hospital and taken to another city. That will happen this afternoon."

Brother swung and walked to the door, opened it and went out, closing the door behind him.

I'll be damned, Harsh thought, wondering how much money was in the packet. His palms suddenly felt sweaty and he rubbed the right one on the sheet. He pulled the money to him and slipped off the rubber band and began to count. He counted off five or six bills and stopped. He took one of the greenbacks with his fingers and held it up to the light, turning it this way and that and speculating on whether it was counterfeit. He did not think it was phony. It was a one hundred dollar bill. His palm was still sweating and he rubbed it on the sheet again, then went on counting, moving his lips and concentrating. Halfway through the pile his hand shook so that he had to pause. Jesus, he thought. He had a coughing spell that wracked him and he wondered if he was out of his goddamn mind. He seized all the money and shoved it under the sheet and lay there breathing heavily. He began to have visions of the nurse coming in and jerking the sheet off him and finding the money and taking it away from him the way they had taken away his clothes. He must be dreaming. Oh hell if he was dreaming, he might as well get the full effect of the dream and finish counting the money. He began counting again and his lips felt very stiff when he tried to move them to frame the numbers. He began to hear the blood going through his ears like water in a faucet. Finally he finished counting the money and clutched it all together and put it under the sheet with him and rolled over on it so the money was under his belly. He lay there having difficulty breathing. He felt the money pushing against the outside of his belly. Then he got the impression the money was penetrating right into his gut and making a lump like a barrel. The lump became as hot as fire. Then it began to melt and as it melted the gold fluid ran through his veins, ran through his veins into his throat, making him sick, making him have to vomit. He did not want to vomit on his bed. He lurched up but he had to let go anyway when he put his weight on his broken arm without thinking and the arm exploded with pain. He had to scream. The scream sounded like a fire engine to his ears. The whole hospital would hear the squall, he thought, and come running to take the money away from him. Oh, Lord. His bed was a mess. So this was how it felt, he thought, to get your hands on fifty thousand dollars.

PART TWO

SEVEN

The cablegram was delivered at eight minutes past ten o'clock that morning and it put real terror into Mr. Hassam. Some minutes passed before he controlled his breathing to the point where he no longer took air into his lungs in shaky gasps. He memorized the name of the town, *Kirksville, Missouri*, where the cablegram had originated, and the name of the hotel, *Colonial Motel*, where the sender wished to be contacted, then he burned the cablegram on his desk ashtray. He sat staring at the ash.

Just burning the cablegram might not be enough, he reflected. You never knew. He kneaded the ashes in his palm to be sure he had thoroughly disposed of them. The paper smoke still hung in the office and it smelled enough like what it was, paper smoke, that anybody chancing to come in might recognize it. The president of the bank, the vice president, a clerk, anyone who came in would know paper smoke when they smelled it, and remember. He supposed anyone at the bank would be afraid to say anything, the situation of the government being what it was. But again, you never knew. Everyone was being careful to keep eyes and ears disconnected from mouths as long as the *descamisada*, the shirtless ones, still thought God had come down to earth and was running the government for their benefit. But the time of crisis was coming.

Since it was only ten o'clock in the morning, Mr.

Hassam thought, God was probably still in bed with one of his teenage friends.

The smoke from the cablegram stank like camel breath, Mr. Hassam reflected, and he got up and opened the window. He stood there looking into the *Avenida del Libertador General San Martin*. It surprised him to see several thousand persons gathered in the street. He could not think what the occasion might be. He could see that the crowd was made up largely of shirtless ones, but for the life of him he could not recall why thousands of the fools should be down there in the street at ten o'clock this morning. He recalled that somewhere in his desk there was a silly calendar made up by some favor-currying concern which showed all the holidays dedicated to *El Presidente* and his late wife. He found the calendar and looked at it. Today was *La Señora De La Esperanza* day, the Lady of Hope Day, which was what the shirtless ones worshipfully called the late wife. So that was it.

Mr. Hassam put away the calendar. He wondered how the project of making a Saint out of *La Señora De La Esperanza* was coming along. *El Presidente* had ordered the Catholics to make his late wife a Saint about a month ago. The Catholic faith was dominant in the country, and the church officials did not like the Saint project. You could not blame them, for she had been a real bitch. It was rumored that *El Presidente* had personally telephoned the Pope in Rome and told him the Saint thing had to go through right away. Mr. Hassam could imagine what a hit that made with the Pope. All those teenage girls he was getting must be giving the bastard a God complex for real, thought Mr. Hassam. If he stirred up all the Catholics, he was opening a hornet nest, and he should have enough sense left to know it.

The way the crowd was starting to gather, there would probably be fifty thousand of them under the lecher's balcony by two o'clock, the hour he usually put in his appearance.

Where was *Kirksville, Missouri*, anyway? In the U.S.A. obviously, since that was where the cablegram had originated. Mr. Hassam was somewhat puzzled as to which was the town and which was the province, and the general location. He consulted an atlas. *Missouri*, he found, was a province in the central U.S.A., and *Kirksville* was a small city.

He still felt frightened. Fear was like having a drink of a strong liquor, vodka or slivovitz or bourbon whiskey, in the way it put a false feeling into a man, and the sensation did not leave the system immediately.

The telephone rang. Mr. Hassam swung about to face the instrument, his nerves tightening. He was reluctant to pick it up, but he felt he must do so.

"Who? Señorita Muirz? Put her on, of course." It was bad business when a man grew frightened at a telephone call, he reflected. "Ah, Miss Muirz. A profound pleasure."

"I plan to be in your office at two o'clock, Hassam."

She sounds high-handed, he thought. He was irritated. High-handedness must be a disease they caught in bed with that bastard. Only last week when he was visiting *El Presidente's* summer residence in Olivos, a teenage flip had ordered Mr. Hassam about as though he were a *peon*, and he had not forgotten.

His voice held its composure. "May I suggest, Miss Muirz, perhaps twelve-thirty would be best for you to come. It is Our Lady of Hope day. The street is already filling with the worshippers."

She laughed. "Very well. Twelve-thirty. Be there. Goodbye."

That was a very nasty little laugh she had given, and he wondered what the Our Lady of Hope worshippers would do if they heard her give it. Tear her limb from limb, he supposed, particularly if they knew she had been *El Presidente's* mistress while his wife was living.

He had better be careful himself, he thought. Flor Muirz was a woman as cold-blooded and calculating as a shark, and she and Doctor Englaster and Mr. Hassam were involved in some promising plans—very promising plans if they were not found out first.

He started walking rapidly around his office. Then he noticed what he was doing. Nerves. He decided to go out for an early lunch. He put on his Panama hat, and because it was quite a hot summer day outside, he took along his palm leaf fan, a rather large fan which he suspected made him look simple-minded. Well, it kept him cool.

When the president of the bank saw Mr. Hassam leaving, he leaped to his feet and hurried out of his glass cage and walked beside Mr. Hassam and opened the street door for him. Mr. Hassam knew the man wanted an invitation to lunch, but he ignored the opportunity. The bank president was always trying to suck up to one of them, either Mr. Hassam, Doctor Englaster, or Miss Muirz, and Mr. Hassam regarded him with distaste. However it was a small thing and not important.

Mr. Hassam went to *La Hermana*, a very nice restaurant, and had a fine lunch. Snails, pressed duck, proper wines, coffee *diablo*, a *Grand Marnier*. The bill was eighty-seven pesos and Mr. Hassam tipped the waiter twenty more, being rewarded with a deep bow. The Panama hat, his fan, were brought him and in accepting them, he returned equal bows. He dawdled before a mirror. He was reluctant to leave, for some reason fancying the peace and security here in the restaurant alone, a touch of sanctuary. The mirror was gilt and full-length, and he noted how his white suit stretched its buttons. The big palm leaf fan did make him look asinine. As a whole he looked like not so much, he reflected, essentially a short, potty and homely pig of a man, about as silly as anything with the fan. He went outside and wedged his way through the growing throng of shirtless ones, many of whom stood with their hands clasped under their chins, praying.

When Mr. Hassam finished counting the money Miss Muirz had brought, he had the total figure as one million three hundred and ninety-four thousand dollars in terms of American money. Miss Muirz sat across the desk taking down the total of each pile as he counted it out. The money for the most part was in Swiss gold franc notes, and Dutch gulden, although there was some U.S. currency. Mr. Hassam arranged the money in piles totaling one thousand U.S. dollars each, using current New York exchange rates in the computation. As ten piles were attained, he stacked them together, since he did not have space for one thousand three hundred and ninety-four piles of one thousand dollars each on his desk.

Mr. Hassam had glanced at Miss Muirz each time he gave her a figure to add to her total, but actually he was preoccupied and hardly conscious of her presence. This was an accomplishment in itself, since there was no lack of manhood in Mr. Hassam. Miss Muirz was something.

Miss Muirz was an exquisitely formed and tawny young woman. Maybe a trifle too tawny, since she had once been a professional *jai alai* player and top money winner at the game, too, and it showed somewhat on her. Whenever she moved there was the impression she flowed like a cat. However, she was lovely. And accomplished. When *El Presidente* was only a Colonel he had stumbled several hours late into an important meeting, and, thoroughly exhausted, had whispered to Mr. Hassam that the woman had given him the goddamn night of his life. Mr. Hassam had only to look at Miss Muirz to believe it. However, manhood was not a factor in Mr. Hassam's mind while better than a million dollars was passing through his hands. The money felt good on his fingers.

Mr. Hassam shuffled together all the piles of ten-thousand, and leaned back. "That should total one million, three hundred and ninety-four thousand." He produced a cigarette. "Would you care to smoke?" He lit her cigarette for her.

Miss Muirz smoked with a long holder, silently, tilting her head slightly to one side to blow out thin streams of smoke.

Mr. Hassam coughed. "I burned a cablegram just before you telephoned. Had I known you were coming, I would not have burned it."

"A cablegram?" Miss Muirz glanced through the smoke at him.

"Yes…from Brother."

She sat bolt upright. "You mean he sent a cablegram directly to you?"

"Yes." Mr. Hassam shuddered. "Yes, he did, and it scared me very much, which is why I lost no time in burning it."

"The fool! He really is quite insane."

"The cablegram said he urgently wanted to talk to one of us on the telephone."

"Oh, Lord. He was such an idiot to do that. He should know. Did he mention any names, Doctor Englaster or myself?"

"No, no names. Poor devil, he has been out of the country five years, out of touch with the situation, so he probably does not know how delicately the sword is balanced over our heads."

"Are you going to telephone, as he wishes?"

"From this country? Not for a million dollars!"

Miss Muirz had brought the money in a suitcase, which Mr. Hassam now placed on his desk. He and Miss Muirz used both hands to scoop the money into it.

Nothing had been said about what Mr. Hassam was to do with the money. The matter had been settled earlier; it was part of an established routine. The money was one month's proceeds from the special import tax levied on machinery imported into the country. By law it was earmarked for the Lady of Hope Memorial Fund for the needy, with *El Presidente* legal custodian of the fund, the latter technicality actually making it his money. It was being invested abroad, as was customary.

Now Miss Muirz handed Mr. Hassam an envelope which he found contained the card the New York banking house required its depositors to fill out. Mr. Hassam smiled at the card approvingly. "Very good indeed." He was referring to *El Presidente's* signature on the card, which was not *El Presidente's* signature at all, but a forgery by Miss Muirz. He slid the envelope and card into his pocket; when he delivered the money to the New York bank, he would turn in the card with the forged signature. This was also customary. However, *El Presidente* had not inaugurated the custom, and knew nothing of it. The substance was that Miss Muirz's forged signature could make a withdrawal, but not *El Presidente's* genuine signature.

It was a bald scheme, and really not as simple as all that.

Mr. Hassam lit another cigarette for Miss Muirz. "Do you suppose Brother, after hunting for nearly five years, has found what he has been seeking?"

She grimaced. "I think Brother grows more unbalanced, just as you think."

"There is not much doubt, I suppose."

Miss Muirz went to the window where she stood smoking and looking down into the street. The street was now almost packed with citizenry.

"*El Presidente* is going to make them a speech at two o'clock, Mr. Hassam. He is going to scare the socks off them. He is going to offer to resign."

Mr. Hassam swung to look at her. He became pale and had to clear his throat. "Resign? Quit the presidency! Oh, Jesus Christ, he cannot do that to us!"

Miss Muirz turned from the window with a smile. "Oh, he does not mean it. He wants to throw his shirtless ones into an uproar, so that they will demand very loudly that he stay in office forever. Then he will promise to do so, but only providing they stand with him against the Pope in Rome."

"But they are all Catholics themselves. They will be promising to fight themselves."

"How many of them have sense enough to think of that? It will stir up a lot of trouble for the Pope."

"Well, I can't see how it can work out for him. He can't whip the Pope in this country."

Miss Muirz laughed outright. "Oh, he has already dismissed the Pope in his mind and is considering taking on God."

Mr. Hassam did not like blasphemy, and he blotted his face with his handkerchief, although he supposed she was right. "I don't know how it will all come out, but none of it is good, because it may bring a crisis before we are ready for it."

"Maybe you had better telephone Brother when you reach a safe place."

"Are you joking again?"

"No, I am not."

Mr. Hassam nodded. "I did not think you were."

Mr. Hassam frequently couriered funds abroad for investment, although he was not the only one who performed such missions. Sometimes Doctor Englaster did it, and sometimes Miss Muirz. Each of them had perfected a procedure. Mr. Hassam's method was to go by car to the airport at Olivos, which was about fifteen miles from the capitol, and from there take this private plane across the Uruguay border to Montevideo, where he obtained airline passage to New York via Miami.

That evening when Mr. Hassam reached Montevideo, he telephoned the airline office and made his reservations to New York, then placed a call to Kirksville, Missouri, U.S.A. The long-distance connection went through very quickly.

"You fool, what are you trying to do, give us all heart attacks?" Mr. Hassam was not afraid of Brother, and he was angry. "Never send me another direct cablegram. Never."

Brother replied mildly. "This was an important matter."

"Nothing is as important as my life where I am concerned. What have you done, found another prospect for a double? This will make about the fiftieth one you have found, will it not?"

"Oh, now, listen. Listen to me, Mr. Hassam. This time I have found the very man."

Mr. Hassam could not be positive over a telephonic circuit of that distance, but he had the impression Brother was quite placid and confident. Could Brother really have found a double for the bastard? Wouldn't that be something. He could hardly believe it.

"How sure are you, Brother?"

"The man has the same physical appearance, almost identical. Really shocking resemblance. Not the scar on the face, but Doctor Englaster knows enough to put on the scar. He has the same blood type. And the man is a crook. A cheap down-at-the-heels crook. He will do anything for a few thousand dollars. His name is Harsh. Walter Harsh."

Mr. Hassam advanced a cautious thought. "How about controlling this man? Can it be done?"

"I have taken care of that. Harsh killed a man accidentally in an automobile chase. I have a witness who will perjure himself to clear Mr. Harsh of blame, or hang him in court if we prefer. We can control this Harsh."

Mr. Hassam found difficulty in keeping his breathing at normal. They had, all of them, been hoping for years to find a physical double for *El Presidente*, and it was embarrassing to recall that in the beginning they had felt such a thing would be easy. It was far from easy. It had been impossible to date. Even though they did not plan to use a man to take *El Presidente's* place until he went into political exile in some other nation, still it was not easy. Mr. Hassam had become personally discouraged, and so, he felt, had Miss Muirz and Doctor Englaster. But Brother, who was not exactly rational at all times, had kept at it with fanatic zeal. If they had a double for *El Presidente*, and if they substituted him for *El Presidente* when the latter fled into exile, then there were millions to be had. Somewhere near sixty-five million, American dollars equivalent, as a matter of fact. It was a lot of honey to taste in a man's mouth, and Mr. Hassam felt himself becoming very excited.

"I will go back and tell the others."

"Mr. Hassam, you do that. I was going to ask you to do that. You tell them to be prepared."

"I will contact you later, Brother."

"Yes, you do that. Contact me, but not here. I am going to be at my home in Palm Beach."

⁂

After changing his airline reservations to a later flight, Mr. Hassam re-crossed the border to the capitol, and drove his own car, a light blue Jaguar, from the Olivos airport into town. He went directly to Doctor Englaster's neurological clinic.

Doctor Englaster stood up and they shook hands. Englaster was a tall man, hawklike, with a personality which Mr. Hassam did not care for. Doctor Englaster was a very arrogant man when things were going well. At such times he gave the impression of regarding everything and everyone around him as so much dirt. Not that he expressed the feeling with words. It was his air.

"Buy you a drink, Doctor?" They had long ago decided there was a chance Doctor Englaster's office was bugged, and this was to let him know the news was private and dangerous.

They went to a bar named *Las Violetas* which had once been third-rate but which had done well on nothing more than the strength of the fact that, in the days when he was only an army man, *El Presidente* had often stopped there. That was before *El Presidente* had a half dozen palaces, twenty sports cars, and a seraglio of teenage girls.

Doctor Englaster ordered vermouth for them both without consulting his companion. Mr. Hassam detested vermouth straight, although he did not mind it in a Manhattan. The way Doctor Englaster ordered vermouth was a small sample of his little arrogant mannerisms.

"Well, Mr. Hassam?"

"What do you think of this thing he is going to pull off today, Doc? Offering to resign?"

Doctor Englaster was not as surprised at the news as Mr. Hassam had been. Mr. Hassam abruptly realized, rather sheepishly, that the speech must have been made, and the resignation threat was old news. Doctor Englaster shrugged. "Well, it will work, of course. The cheers were terrific. The *descamisada* have turned against the church officials."

"Temporarily, don't you mean?"

"Oh, yes, that is how it will work."

"How temporarily?"

"Not for long. He can never take God's place with them. He may think he can. He may be that colossal a fool. But he will not do it."

Mr. Hassam decided not to touch his vermouth. "Here is what I really wanted to talk to you about…Brother says he has found exactly the man he has been seeking for these five years."

Doctor Englaster looked about nervously, and his voice dropped to a whisper. "The hell you say! Is that right? I mean, where did you see Brother? The fool, is he here, with times as they are?"

"Oh, no. He is in a province called Missouri, in the U.S.A. I talked to him by telephone." Mr. Hassam outlined what Brother had told him concerning Harsh.

Doctor Englaster recovered his composure and again assumed his superior air. "I believe we all should have a look at this fellow Brother has found."

"I think so, too." Mr. Hassam pushed the glass of vermouth aside. "Do you have a good excuse for taking a quick trip to Miami?"

Doctor Englaster shrugged. "I had announced a planned vacation in Panama. I can easily disappear on a jungle hunting trip from there for a few days."

"How about Miss Muirz?"

"She comes and goes at will, doesn't she?" Doctor Englaster looked at Mr. Hassam meaningfully and rubbed a thumb and forefinger together as if counting money. "How much are you taking out to add to Our Lady of Hope Memorial Fund this time?"

"In United States money, one million three hundred and ninety-four thousand dollars."

Doctor Englaster's eyes glistened. "The take is dropping off."

"Yes." Mr. Hassam shrugged. "Hardly worth getting hung for."

"That is not a very good joke." Doctor Englaster spoke soberly. "We must be careful. Brother is periodically a paranoiac, not a dependable sort. But he is no idiot. He may indeed have found a double for *El Presidente*. Shall we drink to the possibility?"

Mr. Hassam ignored the vermouth and picked up his glass of water for the toast.

EIGHT

Instead of airliner-style seats, the plane boasted four private staterooms and a lounge furnished with deep chairs, a cocktail bar, and an office equipped with desk and dictating machines and chairs for conferences in midair. The pilot and co-pilot/steward wore puce-colored twill uniforms with every crease an edge and every button fastened, each cap peak set at an acute angle. The two crewmen looked efficient and close-mouthed. The color motif inside the airplane was all in tans and puce. There was a strip of the brown along the outside of the airplane and the interior upholstery was out of the same pot, custom stuff. The puce and tan was touched here and there with gold, a gold edging around the television screen, a gold filigree on the door latches.

The two crewmen helped Walter Harsh up the steps into the plane. He was very weak, but he could walk. Moving about had made him feel better, or at least feel more like he was going to live. He noticed the wrist watch the pilot was wearing had a tan dial with puce hands and gold figures. Jesus, he thought. They lowered him into a comfortable chair and buckled the safety belt about his middle. From the windows he could see the wingtips and parts of the engines. The engines puzzled him, because he saw no propellers. Jet? he wondered. The airplane was some buggy.

Brother came in and sat in an upholstered seat near him and fastened the safety belt. He then waited for the plane to take off, sitting there with his mouth open slightly, tips of teeth showing, waiting almost visibly. Harsh decided the man was uneasy about flying.

A taxicab arrived outside. The co-pilot/steward left the plane and soon returned with a large tan canvas bag from the taxi. Harsh eyed the bag. "That's mine. Is my camera and clothes and stuff in there?"

"Yes, Mr. Harsh."

Harsh leaned back, trying to relax. This was one hell of a thing, he thought, the whole thing from beginning to end. They had sold his car for nineteen hundred dollars, which was a roast, because Harsh had paid four hundred for the iron a year ago and gotten a skinning at that. He was amazed when he signed the assignment form on the back of the certificate of title of the car, and Brother counted nineteen hundred dollars into his hand. He knew nobody had been fool enough to pay nineteen for the old iron, so they were just keeping him happy. He could feel a bulb of sweat move down his spinal column under his shirt, and he knew what was making him sweat. Money. The way money was coming at him, he thought, it would make an iceberg sweat. He looked down at his right arm, realizing he had suddenly formed the habit of keeping it across his chest, the hand pressed where the middle vest button would be, if he wore a vest. Like Napoleon. He tried to recall whether Napoleon kept his right or his left hand tucked in his waistcoat front. He wondered if Napoleon carried fifty thousand dollars taped to the skin of his belly under the hand.

What they were waiting on turned out to be Vera Sue Crosby. A taxicab arrived and Vera Sue got out wearing her new hat, a tight skirt, and a bushy fur stole which was also new and emphasized her round little bottom. The stole was mink-dyed muskrat, her skirt was yellow, her slippers gold-colored with very high heels. She looked like she was headed for the Yukon gold rush, Harsh thought.

He swung around in his chair. "Hey, I don't want that dame around me. She double-crossed me and I don't want any part of her."

"Harsh, you take orders, not give them."

Harsh saw the glazed expression in Brother's eyes, and did not press the matter. The man was afraid of the airplane and was forcing himself to take the flight. The fact that Brother owned such an elaborate private plane and was so nervous about using it indicated what was probably a long-standing psychological battle between the man and the airplane. Let him sweat his own troubles out, Harsh decided.

He pointedly ignored the tentative smile Vera Sue flashed in his direction as she moved to a seat. He had a pretty good idea how she felt. The fancy puce uniforms and the plane had knocked her for a loop and she probably felt as out of place as a blowfly in a perfume bottle. He grinned at the thought, liking the comparison.

The plane now moved quietly out to the runway and took off. It made much less commotion than any plane Harsh had flown in. There was none of the roaring and shaking that characterized airplanes with propellers. The takeoff was smooth as grease.

Harsh watched Brother sit there and hate it. Brother gripped the armrests of his chair and the tendons looked like chalk marks down the backs of his hands. The guy will never be a bird by choice, Harsh reflected.

o

No one had told Harsh they were going to New York,
but he had supposed they were because he recalled the
O-Negative Blood Group Foundation having a New York
address. However the plane flew three or four hours and
when it came down Harsh saw palm trees, the sea in the
distance edged with a white sand beach and what seemed
to be large estates. The plane taxied directly into a large
private hangar, where a brown limousine was parked.
Brother got into the limousine holding a handkerchief to
his mouth. He had bitten his lip badly during the mental
strain of riding through the landing.

The limousine carried them quietly for about half an
hour with the afternoon sun mostly against its back windows. The uniformed pilot drove. The co-pilot had
loaded the luggage in the trunk. Harsh decided the two
served double duty as household staff.

The limousine came to a stop before impressive iron
gates, and the co-pilot got out and unlocked the gates
with a key, waited for the limousine to pass through, then
locked the gates, got back in the car, and gave Brother
the gate key.

Sunlight splintered like diamonds off immaculate
marble and the sparkling glass windows of the mansion
before them. The place should be a library in a small city
park, Harsh thought. The limousine turned left and right
between rows of neatly whitened palm trunks and came
to a halt before a leaded glass marquee. Back of the marquee a stained glass door was surrounded by a filigree of
ironwork.

They unloaded from the limousine and Harsh found

himself able to walk, although he was inclined to be dizzy. The downstairs hall had the faint odor of hyacinth, was floored with mother-of-pearl. The woodwork was Honduran mahogany.

Brother gestured to the co-pilot up a stairway with Harsh's bag. "Your room is that way, Harsh."

There was enough space in the bedroom to turn a small automobile. The bed was all of nine feet wide, one room wall was all glass with the ocean beyond it a crinkling aquamarine panorama to the horizon.

Harsh grinned at Brother, who'd followed him up. "As the fellow says, this ain't exactly what I'm used to."

Brother showed his teeth, which Harsh saw bore a brownish scum from the blood that had come into the man's mouth from biting his lip during the plane's landing. "Your taste does not interest me." He turned to the co-pilot, who had put the bag down by the bed. "Get out."

The man bent his head in an almost imperceptible bow, his eyes lowered and expressionless, then turned and left them.

Harsh glanced at the bed. The bed looked good to him. He was tired, and his broken arm was a bag of pain attached to his shoulder. He went over and gave the bed an experimental poke with his fist. A very good bed.

"The money."

Harsh straightened. Brother had moved silently to his side, stood at his elbow. "Huh?"

"Give the money to me."

Harsh moved his tongue over his lips. He could feel the fifty thousand resting against his solar plexus where he had attached it, along with the nineteen hundred he had received for his car, by the use of hospital adhesive tape. "I thought the money you paid me for my car was mine, and I was to keep it."

Brother tightened his lips over his stained teeth. "Is it necessary you be childish as well as stupid, Harsh?"

"Say now, buddy. Let's not be so free with insults."

"Give me the money."

"Well, now, that needs some talking about. The way I figure, the dough is mine if I do a job, and since I'm doing the job now, why don't we compromise and me keep—"

Brother's neck arched so tensely that his head trembled and his eyes protruded.

Harsh became alarmed. "Keep away from me, you son of a bitch." He knew he did not have the physical strength to put up much of a fight.

Brother leaned toward him. Hit him in the belly, Harsh thought, would be the best move, but hand him a good one so it would settle things. He brought his right fist up toward Brother's middle, but Brother pushed the fist aside easily. Brother lifted his cupped hands and clapped them together against Harsh's ears. The effect on Harsh's eardrums and brain was agonizing. He was sure he had been given a mild concussion. Brother seized Harsh's right arm and turned with the arm so that his back was to Harsh, the thumb and wrist in a trap-hold which was the most painful thing Harsh had ever had anyone put on him. His wrist and thumb filled with splintering pain, until he thought fire would come out of his ears. He toppled backwards onto the bed when Brother released him. He felt Brother tear open his shirt and begin pulling the taped-on money loose from the skin. Brother's eyes shone insanely and he drew the tape loose slowly and agonizingly, panting with pleasure as the tape brought the coarse belly hair out by the roots. When Brother arose, the packet of money was in his hands, all of it, Harsh's nineteen hundred as well as the fifty thousand.

"Mr. Harsh, I give an order only once. I state only fact. I do not threaten, bicker, chisel, or bargain. If any time you hear me make a statement which you wish to construe as a threat, stop. Stop. If I have said it, it is fact, not a threat. A fact beyond recall, unalterable, unassailable, unchangeable, a fact."

"You got my nineteen hundred there!" Harsh was half blinded with pain.

"Get up."

"Damn you!"

"Get to your feet."

Harsh's ears felt as if steam was escaping through them and he wondered if the eardrums were ruptured. When he saw Brother take a step toward him, he hastily rolled off the bed and stood shakily erect. This crazy fool would kill him, like as not.

"Come. I wish to show you something." Brother turned and walked to a framed painting on the east wall of the bedroom. The painting was an oil copy of Titian's *Woman on a Couch*, a very bold and sexy-looking piece. Brother swung the painting outward like a small door. It was hinged to the wall. This disclosed a wall safe with a combination dial.

"Watch, Harsh. Watch closely. Memorize the combination." Brother turned the safe dial slowly to four different numbers, reciting each number aloud. He did this again. "Have you got it, Harsh?"

"I think so."

"Repeat the combination aloud to me to be sure."

Harsh muttered the numbers, and the directions the dial was turned each time.

Brother nodded. "Now watch closely."

The inner door was a flat sheet of steel with two openings for keys. It was similar, Harsh recalled, to safety deposit boxes in some banks. Brother drew two keys from his pocket. They were fastened together by a string. He inserted each key in a lock, swung open the door.

"It takes both keys to open the inner door. You understand, Harsh?"

"I get it."

Brother placed the money in the safe and locked both inner and outer door. He swung the painting back in place. It covered the safe completely. He tore the two keys apart, breaking the string. He put one key in his pocket.

"You get to keep the other key, Harsh."

He handed Harsh the second key.

"Goddamn it, my nineteen hundred is in there too!"

Brother ignored him. "Only these two keys will open the inner door. I keep one. You keep one. When you have earned your pay, I will give you my key. The money is safe. You know where it is."

"What about my nineteen hundred?"

Brother turned and walked to the door, went out, closing the door after him.

Harsh went over and lay on the bed, taking care not to jar the cast that enclosed his left arm. He held the key tightly in his right hand.

NINE

Harsh slept nine hours. He awakened with the notion he had been trying to cry out in frustration and had been grinding his teeth together. His throat felt dry and his jaws hurt. It was dark in the bedroom, no light at all coming from the big window, and he decided someone had come in while he was asleep and closed the drapes over the window.

He again recalled the grinding sensation with his teeth, and he was alarmed. He inserted an exploratory finger in his mouth, finding the key to the wall safe was secure. His teeth must have been crunching on the key as he slept. He had placed the key in his mouth before he went to sleep, not worrying about swallowing it because he often went to sleep with chewing gum in his mouth and he had never swallowed that. He realized, however, he must find a more practical hiding place for the key.

He did not like so much darkness in the room, it made him uneasy. He pushed up to a sitting position on the bed, found the edge, and lowered his feet to the floor. The ringing that had been in his ears when he went to sleep was no longer there. He decided his eardrums had not been ruptured. Shuffling barefoot to the window, he parted the drapes, and a flood of moonlight spilled over him. Beyond the window the moonlight covered a wide sweep of cucumber-green lawn and a rope of lime-colored driveway lined by palm trees that were as motionless as upclenched fists. The moonlight made everything very clear. On the beach, night birds were chasing along a squirming yarn of white surf and beyond to the horizon the sea was a blue-black bedspread with a pattern of crinkling waves.

Harsh rubbed his jaw with his right hand. The place looked peaceful, he thought, but there was something to be said for packing up and getting the hell out. The manhandling he had taken at the hands of Brother had undermined his confidence. He had underestimated Brother. The man had a tough, sadistic streak. His right hand and arm still ached where Brother had worked on him with that judo trick. He was sure Brother had inflicted most of the pain just for the twisted satisfaction of hurting him. He would be goddamned if he was going to stay around here and be handled like raw meat...

But he was also damned if he'd leave before getting that wall safe open. He tried to recall what he knew about wall safes. It was very little. Could a man wedge something into the inner crack of the safe door, he wondered, and get it open?

Suddenly excited, determined to tackle the safe, he went to his suitcase and found the package of blades for his safety razor. He took one blade from the package and went to the painting and swung it back, exposing the safe dial. He blew on his right hand for luck and tackled the dial, turning it carefully to the numbers as he remembered them. It would not open! He grabbed it, shook it. It would not open. The son of a bitch changed the combination on him, he thought, and his stomach felt tight. He rubbed his forehead with his right hand briskly, trying to recollect the combination. He was sure it was the way he had just worked it. He tried it again, exactly the same way.

The safe's outer door opened. He leaned against the wall, sweating with relief. Done some damn little thing wrong, he thought. He wiped his nose on his sleeve before continuing, then gripped the safety razor blade by the edge and attacked the crack. The crack was wide enough to admit the blade, but it struck bottom after penetrating about half an inch, and he could feel nothing like a lock or a bolt. He tried forcing the blade to bend and find its way to the bolt. The blade broke. The hinges were constructed so that he could not get at them. He tried another blade, but this one broke as well, cutting his finger. He gave up and stood there leaning his forehead against the cool metal of the safe.

The thing now, did he leave here without the money, or did he stick around for a break? By God, he would stay, that was what he would do. He would lick the thing yet. He closed the safe and got in bed and pulled the sheet up around his neck.

There was an enormous amount of sunshine in the room when he awakened and felt in his mouth for the key. He wondered what would happen if he sneezed or something in his sleep and swallowed the key. How did one get a key out of one's stomach? How about a magnet? He examined the key and saw it was brass, which was non-magnetic. He had better find a place for the key, that was what he had better do.

A knock sounded on the door. Throwing the door open, Brother rolled in a small metal cart bearing breakfast, an omelet, coffee, and toast. Brother glanced at Harsh with an expression of dislike, and he did not speak. He left without having said a word.

Have to go back to the device of securing the key to his body somewhere with adhesive tape, Harsh reflected, since he was too damn dumb to think of another disposition for it. He couldn't go around with the thing in his mouth. He went into the adjoining bathroom, which had a step-down tub, separate shower, ultra-violet light cabinet, and an electric massage device. He searched for adhesive tape, but was unable to find any. He wondered what you were supposed to do around here if you barked a shin, call a servant or something?

He went back and peered at the breakfast Brother had brought him. The omelet had bits of green herbage in it and he peered at this suspiciously, wondering if it was edible. He would not be a bit surprised to have Brother try to poison him, the way the bastard looked at him every time he came around.

He ate the toast and drank the coffee, then took a tentative bite of omelet. It tasted fine. It was better than any omelet he had ever eaten, in fact, as well as different.

He lay back, feeling stronger for having eaten, more relaxed, and sure he wasn't licked yet on the safe problem. He would figure something. One way or another, he would get into that safe. And until he got the job done, he was not going to allow the safe out of sight if he could help it.

He wondered if he just lay there in bed and stared at

the wall safe, how long it would be before something came into his head that would get the inner door of the thing open.

He watched the safe all that day.

He watched it most of the next night, tossing sleeplessly.

TEN

The airliner from South America put down for its sched-
uled Caribbean refueling stop, taking on 100 octane gas,
giving the passengers a few minutes to stretch legs and
buy souvenirs. Mr. Hassam gained confidence he was not
being trailed, watching the fellow travelers. But he would,
he decided, stay with a policy of caution, not getting off
at Miami, which was the short route to Brother's home in
Palm Beach, but going on to New York and doubling
back. You never knew. Also Miami was dangerous. Many
exiles, unfriendly to *El Presidente*, were in Miami, and
since it was more or less known that he was a private
courier for *El Presidente*, an embittered expatriate might
take a shot at him just for the satisfaction. They were a
bitter lot, those exiles, and they would like nothing better
than to pot a treasury courier.

The stewardess offered to put Mr. Hassam's large suitcase with the other passenger baggage.

"No, no, Miss." Mr. Hassam shook his head firmly.
"No, thank you." He smiled at the stewardess and told
her his little joke. "I have my life preserver with me in the
suitcase, you know."

Later the airliner skirted the east coast of Florida. It
flew at high altitude but the day had crystal clarity, and Mr.
Hassam was able to distinguish Brother's mansion among
the string of elaborate estates facing the sea near Palm
Beach. He was very curious. What was the story down

there, he wondered. Had Brother found their man, really?

The arrival in New York was uneventful. Mr. Hassam, never letting the suitcase out of hand, crossed New York City in a succession of taxicabs, entering a cab and riding thirty blocks or so and suddenly dismissing that cab to take another in a different direction, arriving eventually at Teterboro Airport across the Hudson River in New Jersey. Here he chartered a small fast plane to Pittsburgh, from which point he chartered another small plane to Palm Beach.

At Palm Beach, he took another taxicab. The suitcase rode in the seat beside him. He had not deposited the money in the New York bank. That would come later, after the matter of the fingerprints was settled. If they were going to add forged fingerprints to the forged signatures, then this shipment was as good a place as any to start.

Before leaving South America, Doctor Englaster, Miss Muirz, and Mr. Hassam had set up a pre-arranged meeting place. The Indian River Palms, a motel.

Mr. Hassam found Miss Muirz and Doctor Englaster at the Indian River Palms registered in different cottages. He did not ask them by what route they had arrived, and they did not question him.

"Have you contacted Brother?"

Doctor Englaster nodded. "By telephone, yes. We are to come out. He has the man here, he says."

"How did he sound? I mean his mental health? Stable? You do not suppose this is all a delusion?"

"I do not know a better way to find out than to go out there." Doctor Englaster was wearing his superior manner.

❖

Brother himself unlocked the iron gate for them, running to them with outstretched hand. "Ah, my friends! My wonderful friends!"

Mr. Hassam watched him closely, for he halfway expected to find Brother as crazy as a loon. Brother hailing them as his wonderful friends did not bolster Mr. Hassam's confidence, since Brother was notoriously unfond of Miss Muirz. But it developed Brother had not at first noticed Miss Muirz in the car. He brought up at sight of her, controlling himself with obvious effort.

Brother shook hands with Mr. Hassam and Doctor Englaster, but not Miss Muirz. "How are things at home?"

Doctor Englaster opened the car door for Brother to get in with them for the short ride to the house. "Getting ready to blow up with a bang from indications."

"I gathered as much from the newspapers here. How much time do we have?"

"Who knows. The fuse is lit, that is sure. A few weeks at the outside, I would say, maybe less."

"Time enough." Brother waved them under the marquee at the house. "This man I have found, this Harsh, he is perfect. You shall see."

"Does he know what he is to do? Have you told him?"

"Not yet. I wanted you to inspect him first."

"Is Harsh cooperative?"

Brother gave a mirthless laugh. "I am making a cooperator out of the fellow. I gave him fifty thousand dollars to show him his pay, then took it away from him and locked it in the wall safe in his room. He has been lying there on the bed in his room for two days watching the safe like a mongrel dog trying to figure how to dig up a buried bone."

Mr. Hassam exchanged glances with Doctor Englaster and Miss Muirz. Brother's sanity might be questionable after all. Mr. Hassam felt a strong wish to meet this Harsh person. It might be that Brother's method was exactly the one to work on Harsh, in which case it was sensible.

They encountered Vera Sue Crosby on the terrace. Brother had not planned the meeting. Beside the lounge chair on which Vera Sue lay was a Benedictine bottle and a glass, both in use. Vera Sue wore a dab of yellow sunsuit, and she was glad to see them, for she was lonesome. She was only a slight bit tipsy. She got up and shook their hands warmly when Brother introduced them as Señor Tomas, Señor Ricardo, and Señorita Maria, friends of his. Vera Sue was ignorant of Spanish and did not know he had presented them as Tom, Dick, and Mary, and she asked them to have a drink with her, which they declined.

"Oh, have a pick-up after your trip. I'm sure glad to see a new face around here. This place has been like a damn morgue."

Brother declined for them, got Vera Sue back in the lounge chair with a glass in her hand, and they moved on. "She is Harsh's *sillero*." Brother's lips curled with contempt. "A nothing."

Benedictine at ten o'clock in the morning, my God, Mr. Hassam was thinking. But a well-stacked little trollop.

Doctor Englaster smiled with superior amusement. "Why did you bring her here, may I ask?"

"She knew a little, and I was not sure when a little might become too much."

Doctor Englaster suddenly looked appalled. "Do we have to cut her in on the loot?"

"Are you mad?"

Miss Muirz had said nothing, just looked Vera Sue over speculatively. "Having seen this Harsh's taste in girl-friends, I have a suggestion. I believe he is susceptible. Suppose I see him first."

An exchange of glances passed among the three men. It was a hell of a good idea, Mr. Hassam thought. One encounter with Miss Muirz and Harsh would have difficulty knowing whether he was coming or going.

Miss Muirz left them to visit Harsh.

Mr. Hassam heard Brother cursing softly in Spanish, his eyes closed, his voice low and furious. He was calling Miss Muirz all the Spanish words that even remotely meant bitch.

Except to serve him breakfast, no one had visited Harsh that morning, not that he cared. He was watching the wall safe with the dull malevolent fury of a lion in a trap. He had been able to think of no way into the safe. Repeated efforts to pick the lock had failed. Now he was lying back glowering in what amounted to a self-induced trance.

When the door opened and someone came in, he did not look around. He thought it was Brother until a whiff of excellent perfume touched his nostrils, when he concluded it was Vera Sue. The greedy little slut!

"Listen, Vera Sue, get the hell out of here—"

His visitor laughed, and he turned his head. He sat erect as if he had been lifted by the eyeballs.

"Gee, I'm sorry, Miss."

"Good morning, Mr. Harsh. You are Mr. Harsh, I presume."

"Uh-huh. I thought you were somebody else."

"I am Flor Muirz."

"Well, I'm Walter Harsh, Miss Muirz, the pieces that are left of him. And say now, I can see where the pieces might grow back together in a hurry now you're here."

He was taking Miss Muirz in from head to toe. She was a long graceful girl with a big roll of hair on the top of her head that was so blonde that it had a neon light quality.

"Would you like some coffee, Mr. Harsh?"

"Why, yes, sure, thanks. Say, I don't see how on earth I mistook you for Vera Sue."

"Don't let it bother you, Mr. Harsh."

He grinned. "Well, making a mistake like that would indicate I was going blind or something, but I'll try not to let it worry me."

Miss Muirz smiled and brought him a cup of coffee on a tray with sugar and cream. He held his head up off the pillow, watching the skirt skate around on her hips. It became some trouble for him to keep the coffee cup in place on the saucer.

"Say, you're not going to be my nurse, by any chance?"

"I'm not a nurse, Mr. Harsh."

"Oh. I wouldn't have that kind of luck, anyway."

She laughed. "I don't know. Maybe I could be your part-time nurse, if you need one."

"I'm not sure if that would kill or cure me."

She poured herself a cup of coffee and sat on the edge of his bed. She drank with him. The expensive odor of her perfume affected his breathing. From the corner of an eye he could see where the cloth of her skirt was drawn tightly across her thigh a few inches from his face, and he began to think what a hell of a place that would be to take a good bite. His chest felt tight.

"How is your arm, Mr. Harsh? I believe I was told it was broken."

"Yeah, it got mashed between two cars."

"How is it mending?"

"All right, I guess. Nobody has said different. You say your name is Muirz? How do you spell that?"

She gave him the spelling. "I'm pleased you are on the mend."

"What kind of name is that, Muirz?"

"I am South American."

"I figured. You had a little bit of an accent or something."

"Would you like me to read aloud to you, Mr. Harsh?"

"Huh? Read to me?" Being read aloud to might have been the one thing farthest from Harsh's thoughts. "Read to me? Well, I hadn't thought of that."

"You look tired, and being read aloud to is often soothing."

"Sure, read to me if you want to." Harsh could not remember anyone ever having read to him aloud.

Miss Muirz began reading aloud to him from Spinoza, which proved baffling for Harsh. He had never heard of Spinoza. Miss Muirz took the book from her purse. It was *Ethics, First Part, Concerning God, with Definitions*.

"*I. By cause of itself, I understand that, whose essence involves existence; or that, whose nature cannot be conceived unless existing. II. That thing is called finite in its own kind which can be limited by another thing of the same nature. For example, a body is called finite, because we always conceive another which is greater. So a thought is limited by another thought; but a body is not limited by a thought, nor a thought by a body. III. By substance, I understand that which is in itself and is conceived through itself; in other words, that the conception of which does not need the conception of another thing from which it must be formed."*

Harsh listened with a blank expression. Jesus, he thought, who had ever heard of such stuff being sprung on a man. However, Miss Muirz had a reading voice that was low and cultured and musical, and her dress had an interesting way of snuggling up when she took a deep breath so that her nipples stuck out at him. But he did not care greatly for Spinoza.

Mr. Hassam jumped to his feet in the library when Miss Muirz joined them. He was irritated because she had been gone nearly an hour. He was tired from the trip, and he wanted to have a look at Harsh himself, then get some sleep. Doctor Englaster had expressed himself as feeling the same way. Neither of them hated Miss Muirz the way Brother did, but neither of them liked her much either.

Doctor Englaster spoke with sarcasm. "Really, you take longer to weave your spells nowadays, don't you?"

Miss Muirz shrugged. "I weave well-made goods, Doctor."

"So I have heard."

Watch out, Doc, Mr. Hassam thought, watch what you say to her. She is not a patient soul like I am and if she should get her fill of you, then you are likely to be in trouble.

"How did Mr. Harsh impress you, Miss Muirz?" Mr. Hassam spoke hastily.

"Perfect."

"How did you get along with him? Can he be handled?"

"I think so. He reacts normally. I gave him an over-dose of sex, followed by an overdose of culture—in other words, I waved my bottom at him, then read to him aloud from Spinoza. Yes, I would say he reacts normally."

Mr. Hassam considered the combination of Miss Muirz's bottom and Spinoza, and he wondered how Harsh had survived.

Doctor Englaster spoke sharply. "And you think this man will do for our purpose?"

"Perfectly." There was a strange look in Miss Muirz's eyes. "He even has *El Presidente's* dirtily eager way with women."

Walter Harsh took a quick liking to Mr. Hassam and oddly enough it was for reasons which Mr. Hassam preferred to be appreciated. Mr. Hassam walked into the room and Harsh looked at him, seeing a roundly firm short man with pale coffee skin and a large nose the prominent item in a set of homely features. The full-blown mobile lips, the large innocent eyes, were not impressive.

But Mr. Hassam at once did a thing which set him in solid with Harsh. What Mr. Hassam did was give the wall safe a knowing glance, then wink at Harsh. He did this so the others did not observe. It had the same effect on Harsh that an orator is striving for when he opens his speech with a gut-buster joke. It warmed up the audi-ence, got it interested. The little smoky guy might be an operator, Harsh thought.

Brother made introductions. "Señor Hassam. Doctor Englaster." He shrugged and added, "My associates."

The first impression Harsh got of Doctor Englaster was the same one that Mr. Hassam had formed after long acquaintance. The man liked to smell of himself. Harsh noted Doctor Englaster was impressive physically, a man taller than himself by several inches, with well-proportioned shoulders and arms, and smooth flexible looking hands. The well-fitting clothes, the good grooming, meant the man had been successful for a long time. Harsh did not think he would ever be buddy-buddy with the man.

Doctor Englaster did the talking.

"How are you, Harsh? Physically, I mean."

"Okay, I guess, considering. Making progress, anyhow."

"I should like to examine you." Doctor Englaster's English was good, very Oxford.

"You're a real doc?"

"Yes."

"Are you a head-shrinker?"

"I beg your pardon?"

"Are you a psychiatrist or whatever they call it?"

"As a matter of fact, yes." Doctor Englaster, who was indeed a practicing psychiatrist, wondered how Harsh had guessed it. Brother had indicated Harsh was a mental oaf, which could be an error. "Psychiatrists are, as you may know, also medical doctors. It is as a medical doctor that I wish to examine you."

"You mean my arm?"

"Well, yes, the arm. But a complete physical inspection also."

Doctor Englaster was *El Presidente's* personal physician, and the purpose of going over Harsh was to search for scars, old bone fractures, or other items which might indicate Harsh was an imposter. But Doctor Englaster was not going to tell Harsh this was his reason.

"Are you going to be my regular doctor?"

"Conceivably so, if I decide you are acceptable."

The remark made no hit with Harsh. He had decided he did not like Doctor Englaster.

"Well, goddamn it, you don't need to act like it was veterinary work."

The three conspirators conferred with Brother in the second floor solarium following Harsh's physical examination.

"Well?" Brother looked to them for opinions.

"I could swear the man is *El Presidente*." Miss Muirz seemed dazed. "It is literally inconceivable."

Doctor Englaster fitted a cigarette in a very long platinum holder. "The man does not speak a word of Spanish." He was not very fond of Harsh either. "That is a serious obstacle."

Brother shrugged. "Nothing."

"The exiled president of a South American country who cannot speak a word of Spanish?" Doctor Englaster's eyebrows shot up. "That is nothing? Why, it is preposterous, man."

Miss Muirz was shaking her head. "No. Harsh can manage. When *El Presidente* goes into exile, he will be afraid of assassination. He will allow no Spanish-speaking strangers near him."

Mr. Hassam thought the same thing. "*El Presidente* is sure to take another identity, pretend to be someone else, when he first goes into exile. That is where Harsh can step in. We can get away with it."

Doctor Englaster frowned. "What about the teeth? Dental records are a means of identification, just as are blood types and fingerprints."

"They made X-rays of Harsh's teeth at the hospital. Those X-rays are no longer in the hospital's files." Brother smiled at Doctor Englaster. "It will be very simple. *El Presidente's* personal dentist is connected with your clinic, is he not?"

"Yes, but—"

"You will substitute Harsh's X-rays for the genuine X-rays of *El Presidente's* teeth."

They fell silent. Mr. Hassam imagined each of them enjoying the same greedy line of thinking. They had worked for years falsifying those signatures on *El Presidente's* investments abroad, working with the open-faced daring of a traveling salesman juggling two wives, hoping they could eventually find a man to serve as a figurehead for *El Presidente* long enough to enable the conspirators to liquidate the foreign deposits, now amounting to some sixty-five million, and make off with the money. It was a fabulous scheme. The possibility of its imminent fruition filled them all with the same heat.

"He still speaks no Spanish." Doctor Englaster moved the flame from a jeweled lighter in front of his cigarette. "It is a liability."

"Did you know, Doctor, I was once a language professor?" Mr. Hassam got to his feet. "Suppose I test his linguistic aptitude. Who knows? If it is favorable, I may be able to cram enough Spanish into him to get him by."

Harsh's initial good opinion of Mr. Hassam improved further when the fat man wheeled in a cart on which was an assortment of liquor bottles, ice, seltzer. Mr. Hassam, a man who noticed things, had remembered that Vera Sue Crosby had been drinking Benedictine and he had included a squat bottle of this, but Harsh said he preferred bourbon, straight. Mr. Hassam poured a pair. They clinked glasses.

"Harsh, I am going to ask you some questions, and have you make some sounds. If you wish to think I have a hole in the head, just go right ahead and think it."

"All right by me, Hassam. Thanks for bringing in something to drink."

"What I am actually going to do is test your aptitude for learning the Spanish language, Harsh. Do you know what vowels are?"

"Vowels? You mean A, E, I, O, U? I got that crap in school."

"Good. You are familiar with what consonants are?"

"I guess."

"Give me some examples."

"I guess I ain't that familiar with consonants, Mr. Hassam."

"Did you graduate from college, Harsh?"

"Not exactly."

"From high school?"

"Not exactly that, either."

"The eighth grade?"

"I got four months into the eighth grade. Me and the teacher didn't seem to jibe."

"Don't worry about it. Now, you will repeat after me: *La cabeza es para pensar*. Will you repeat that? Get the sounds as nearly the same as mine as you can."

"Law caboose is a pair pants, sir."

"Come come, Harsh, no joking. This is important. It is in the nature of an important test. I can tell you that you have passed nearly all other requirements. This is the one remaining test, and believe me, Harsh, it is an essential one. Now say after me: *La boca es para hablar*."

"*La boca es para hablar*."

"Oh, excellent. Much better. Much. Again, please. Watch the stress on the same syllables as I placed it. Again."

Harsh made the sounds requested time after time, matching Mr. Hassam's patience with a tolerant curiosity. They had another round of bourbon together. Mr. Hassam then gave a lengthy speech about Harsh being handicapped by unfamiliarity with the psychological make-up of the national character of the Spanish-speaking people in South America, stating this was an unfortunate handicap because the real character of a language stemmed from the user's environment and habits, and unless one knew the character and environment, preferably knew it firsthand and from experience, then a man would encounter difficulty with the finer nuances of handling the speech of the land, and in particular of the individual who was supposed to be speaking, although as a whole it was not an insurmountable thing if a man applied himself judiciously. Following this out of a clear sky, Mr. Hassam asked Harsh to repeat all the words he had been pronouncing earlier. Harsh came back, getting all of them out, not muffing the pronunciation very seriously.

"Good, oh good for you! Far better than I expected." Mr. Hassam did not conceal his delight.

"Did I pass, Professor?"

"Oh, excellent."

"Well, as the fellow says, you didn't catch me at my best today. To tell the truth my head is kind of fuzzy from the shots I been getting for the pain in my arm." He did not mention the sleeplessness from watching the wall safe.

Mr. Hassam conveyed his favorable impression to the others in emphatic terms. "I vote for this man. I tell you, I have had my doubts about the sanity of this project from time to time. But not now. This man can pull it off. We will never find a better candidate."

Miss Muirz nodded. "I am sure."

Doctor Englaster hesitated. "There is the matter of the broken arm the fellow has."

"It will mend."

"Suppose it does not?"

Mr. Hassam shrugged. "Then *El Presidente* will just have to break his arm when he flees into exile. A broken arm will be believable, I imagine. He will be fortunate if he does not collect a hide full of bullets."

"I hope not." Brother's eyes were suddenly nasty. "I want to shoot the bastard myself."

Miss Muirz looked away suddenly. Her eyes focused rigidly on nothing in particular.

Doctor Englaster eyed Brother. "You are sure of the blood type?"

"Positive. The same as *El Presidente*, O-negative. I checked it twice."

Doctor Englaster waved his long cigarette holder. "You know, I think the bounder might do."

Harsh had never been fingerprinted by the police. His encounters with the punitive side of the law either had not been on charges sufficiently serious to warrant printing or had been in smaller communities where the police did not go in for promiscuous printing. He had been fingerprinted when taken into the army, however. He assumed his prints were on file with the Pentagon or the FBI or wherever they kept them. He thought of all this quickly when Mr. Hassam asked him to put his fingerprints on a card. By the time he decided not to object, Mr. Hassam had the card and ink pad ready, and he took hold of Harsh's hand.

"Hey, Mr. Hassam, let's see the card. That's kind of a funny-looking fingerprint card, ain't it?"

Mr. Hassam smiled faintly. He gave Harsh the card. Harsh had never seen a similar card, having had no occasion to truck with banks handling large deposits, but the printed matter told him it was a bank identification card for filling out by a depositor.

"Mr. Hassam, I put my fingerprints on this thing, what am I getting into?"

"I would not mislead you, Harsh. As soon as your fingerprints are on this card, some money is going to be deposited in the bank using the card for future identification."

"Yeah? How much money?"

"A useful sum, Harsh."

"Will my name be on the card?"

"No. Just your fingerprints."

"Then the money won't be for me?"

"No."

"How much money, Mr. Hassam?"

"Harsh, I do not think I am supposed to tell you that."

"Goddamn it, you want my fingerprints on that card, don't you?" Harsh turned wheedling. "Look, you and I are hitting it off pretty good, Mr. Hassam, so why don't you go all the way?"

"One million three hundred and ninety-four thousand dollars."

Harsh lay back on the bed. He felt he was going to be sick.

"May I take your fingerprints, Harsh?"

"Jesus Christ," Harsh had difficulty breathing. "Go ahead." He let Mr. Hassam take his limp fingers and roll them on the ink pad, then on the card.

"Thank you, Harsh."

"Mix me another slug, will you?" Harsh's voice was ragged. "You people are going to ruin my health, did you know that?" He closed his eyes, did not open them when Mr. Hassam placed a glass half full of bourbon in his fingers.

Mr. Hassam carried the card into the solarium. He waved it under the noses of his confederates.

Doctor Englaster frowned. "Didn't Harsh object to giving you his fingerprints?"

"I gave him a verbal anesthetic." Mr. Hassam smiled.

Harsh was sitting up in bed, another drink in his hand, looking at the wall safe when Doctor Englaster came into his room.

This is the stuck-up son of a bitch, Harsh thought.

"What do you want, head-picker?"

"I have a piece of information for you, Harsh."

"I wish you had sent Miss Muirz in to tell it to me."

"Miss Muirz is busy."

"I bet she could be kept busy, all right." Harsh was somewhat drunk. "How about you taking Miss Muirz a little message from me saying that if she wants to get real busy, she should come in here and see me."

Doctor Englaster's cheeks were beginning to flatten out. "Miss Muirz will visit you at her own convenience, I imagine."

"Is that so? Well, is that a sample of the goddamn hospitality around here? Is that what it is?"

"If you wish anything in the way of food or drink, I imagine you can get it by ringing."

"Just ring, huh, Doc? Okay, I'll ring or rub the lamp, or something. I would rub you, only I can see you're not Aladdin's lamp."

"You do that."

"Doc, you snoot-up bastard, what's with this Muirz?"

"I do not believe I understand."

"Oh, you understand me. Between us boys, what's with that babe? To start with, who does she climb into the hay with around here?"

"Mr. Harsh!"

"Can it, Doc. You can *Mr. Harsh!* me all you want, you won't convince me you haven't eyed that piece yourself. And if she's off limits, I bet you know who it is that's keeping her that way." He took another swallow of his drink. "You know what I think? I think he may not be packing enough for her, whoever he is."

"May I suggest you are drinking and talking overly much, Harsh?" Doctor Englaster controlled his anger. "You need to be in good physical condition for your operation tomorrow."

"I know it ain't you that's disappointing her, Doc. It ain't you because I don't think you pack enough to even start the disappointment." Harsh paused and blinked his eyes carefully. "What was that last?"

"Tomorrow morning I am going to put that scar on your face."

"You are? On me?" Harsh rolled his eyes. "Old Scarface Wally Harsh, I'm to be knowed as, huh?" Suddenly Harsh sat up yelling. "You ain't goin' to cut on my face, you son of a bitch. Not until I get that money back in my hands!" He endeavored to throw his glass of whiskey at Doctor Englaster but it slipped out of his fingers and fell on the bed where he could not find it in the covers.

ELEVEN

Harsh lay quietly on the bed. For almost an hour he hardly moved. Then the liquor stimulated his kidneys and he got up and went to the bathroom. He was still tipsy enough to be sure that he had to be very precise about each thing he did, and he made the decision that he was precisely scared, that was what he was. His face even looked scared in the bathroom mirror. That sweat on his upper lip was not from the heat.

He addressed himself in the mirror. "What did you put your damn fingerprints on that card for?" His voice sounded scratchy and dry. "Man, you didn't think, that's what you didn't do." He cleared his throat of phlegm and spat it in the sink. "One million three hundred ninety-four thousand dollars." He looked at himself. His mouth was hanging open. "Dumb bastard. Somebody's kidding you, you dumb bastard."

He laid his fingers against his left cheek and pulled the skin down then pushed it up. He decided the face suited him the way it was, without a scar. He did not want any scar on his face. Someone must be kidding him about the scar too. That was what they had been doing, joshing him, and he was joshing back when he gave permission to do it. Hey, had he told anybody they could carve a scar on him? Great God, he was out of his head if he had told anyone they could scar him.

His right arm gave him a stab of pain when he lowered it. That Brother had just about torn his arm off with that judo stuff, and had looked as if he wanted to laugh like hell while he was doing it. The man liked inflicting pain. When they got ready to cut a scar on his face, Brother would enjoy throwing him down and sitting on him while they did it.

If Harsh didn't want to know how that felt, he had better get out of this dump.

He ran into the bedroom and glared at the wall safe. The dirty, dirty, dirty bastard, putting all his money in the safe and then locking it with two keys and giving him one key to tantalize him.

He glanced at the window and saw it was night outside. The bright Florida moonlight was shining in the window. Night, he thought, was the time to slip away from here because nobody would see him. *But how far would I get with no money?* What the hell would it take to open that safe anyway? Would a pickaxe do it? A pickaxe was quite a tool if you put the oof in it when you swung it, and an estate this size would have a tool house somewhere and in the tool assortment might be a pickaxe. But he only had one arm. And the noise. He thought of the noise a pickaxe would make. It was a bum idea, the pickaxe. He would have to come up with a better one than that. The thing to do was lie down and bat his brains until something came out. Maybe he could get up his nerve to rob somebody in the house and skip with whatever he got. He couldn't leave without a cent, that was for sure.

He turned toward the bed. His eye caught the bottle of Benedictine on the liquor cart, and he brought up short. He began to nod drunkenly to himself. "She got five hundred from Brother, she's bound to have some left." His voice had a vicious note. He picked up the bottle of Benedictine and shuffled to the door. He opened the door and hung his head out in the hall, then set out for the door of Vera Sue Crosby's bedroom.

Vera Sue wore a sheer green silk nightgown which fit tightly to her hips and breasts and loosely elsewhere. She had not been able to sleep either. She was sitting in a low armchair, her feet stuffed in her oldest pair of gold-embroidered mules.

"Oh, hello, Walter."

"I been thinking about you so hard I can't sleep, Vera Sue. Can I come in?"

"Well now I don't know, Walter. You have been acting like you were real mad with me."

"I know. I been feeling sorry about that. I been laying in my room for hours trying to think of how to make up with you, but I couldn't think of any way. So I just decided to come over. How about having a drink of water with me, at least?"

Sharing a drink of water was a long-standing joke with them. "Well, I guess you can come in, Walter."

He entered and closed the door. The bedroom was elaborate to the point of being ridiculous, the furniture Louis XIV silk brocades, the woodwork carved and painted and gold-leafed. He knew Vera Sue would love it.

"You know, I like seeing you in a place like this, Vera Sue. Being in a room like this, baby, a real fine room like this, is what you should have. All the time I been laying there trying to think of a way to make up for how I acted, I wished I could give you something like this, a room that was nice enough for you, and here you were in the room all the time. Ain't that a coincidence?"

"You have been drinking, Walter."

"Yeah, I guess I was trying to whiskey-drown the son of a bitch that is me. But you know something, I was too big a son of a bitch for drowning in anybody's whiskey."

"I'm sort of glad you come, Walter. I been mad at you, but I been lonesome as hell."

"I'm glad I came."

"I'm glad you remembered I like Benedictine."

"I'm glad I remembered."

"I had some left, but it was all right for you to bring yours. I been getting up every little bit and having a nip."

"To look at you, Vera Sue, I wouldn't know you had been drinking any."

"A whole bottle tonight, Walter. I drank a whole bottle, one of them big bottles like that one, Walter. The whole bottle."

"You sure carry it well."

"Do I? You have been drinking too, haven't you? Did you say you had? You carry it well too, Walter."

"We both carry everything pretty well, don't we?"

He poured some Benedictine in two water glasses and Vera Sue drank hers rapidly. The little bitch goes after the stuff like it was Tom Collins, he thought. When you drank Benedictine the way you were supposed to, he knew a glass was supposed to last half an hour or so. He was glad she had been hitting the stuff before he got there, though. He wouldn't need as long to get her real tight.

"Walter, can you tell me why we're here? Nobody talks to me. Act like I was measles, that's what they do. And you know something, I'm beginning to feel like I was in jail in the damn place."

"I guess I been poor company."

"Walter, I'm getting scared."

"Well, Jesus take us, baby, I didn't dream you were worried. I thought you knew what was going on. I thought Brother told you. The son of a bitch, I told him to tell you that we were partners in the thing. I told Brother, look, I said, there's a good straight kid, that Vera Sue, and what I get, she gets half of. Either count her in for half or count me out, that's what I said."

"Count me in what, Walter?"

"Why, it's simple as hell. I invented a new kind of film emulsion. Big money deal. Brother is the bankroll. He's going to manufacture the film for me."

Vera Sue moved from the chair to the bed. She sat on the edge of the bed and rubbed her face with her hands, frowning. "I didn't know you were an inventor, Walter."

"Yeah, I ain't a very hot one, but I'm an inventor. Took me one hell of a time to work it out. I been fooling with it since I was a kid, or anyway for years." He wanted to stop lying and start laughing. He could hardly keep a straight face. She was taking it all in—he was a photographer and therefore he knew enough to invent a film emulsion, something that real scientists probably worked on for years, and mostly failed at besides. "Vera Sue, this film emulsion I invented, it is a kind of ultraviolet emulsion, which is a little more high-powered than the infrared. What it does, you take a picture of a person with it, it shows the type of blood they got. That was what all the stink about that O-negative blood was about. Tell you the truth, I didn't know the film was that good when I invented it, and maybe I wouldn't have known, only this Brother got the detective from Kansas City investigating me and that tipped me off I had something. I guess he would have stole my invention if I hadn't got wise, but I did get wise, and I put it up to him cold gosling, and here we are."

"Walter."

"Yeah?"

"Is all that the truth?"

"Jesus Christ, you think I could think up a lie like that?"

"Well, then, I guess there is no need for me to be scared and feel like a prisoner, is there, Walter?"

"Not a bit. Here, how about a kiss?"

"Okay. Just one kiss, though."

He pushed his mouth against hers and presently she dug her teeth into his lip. The Benedictine slopped out of her glass on her hand and she threw glass and all in the air. Benedictine showered down on them. "Bite me back, Walter. But not too hard." He found out that having only one hand was quite a handicap. She finally took off the gown herself lying on the bed and writhing and squirming out of the garment, then throwing the gown up in the air the way she had tossed the liquor. The gown swirled around above them and fell back to the floor, skating from side to side in the air the way a leaf falls. The light fell across her body giving it a glow like cream. Her nipples were like acorns and hurt his chest through his shirt. "Goddamn you, Walter, you still got your shoes on."

When he was sure she was asleep he got out of bed. He leaned down and gave her shoulder a gentle push and she rolled over on her back, her heavy breathing changing to snoring. He grinned. That was what he wanted her to do, snore. It was not hard to get her to snore. She was a snoring machine, this babe, he thought. Now, if she stopped snoring he would know she had awakened and be warned.

Her purse had seven dollars in bills and some change. He took it. He had seen her hide her money too many times when she was tight to need to waste time hunting. He went directly to her best pair of slippers in the closet. It was there, in the toes of the slippers, divided about half and half. He counted it.

"Jesus!"

There was twenty-two dollars. He knew she had gotten five hundred from Brother for selling him the names of the references. Could she have blown it all? She must have. She had frittered away all but twenty-nine dollars and forty-four cents. He counted it carefully. Stupid bitch. Stupid, stupid, stupid. How could she blow every cent she got her paws on?

Harsh lurched to the bed, where Vera Sue lay sleeping loudly, a succession of resonant snores coming from her lips. He reared back and socked her across the jaw with his fist. Her arms jerked and threw the covers askew. The snores stopped. He looked at his hand angrily. Skinned the hell out of his knuckles. On his way out the door, he began to suck on his knuckles.

TWELVE

Doctor Englaster came into Harsh's room about ten the next morning dressed for the operation as is customary for surgery, white gown and skullcap, surgeon's mask, rubber gloves. His large flexible hands looked like bunches of bananas in the yellow gloves. Mr. Hassam rolled in an operating table improvised from a massage table, and Miss Muirz pushed in a smaller service table bearing instruments and medicants and a bright light for the operation. Harsh watched the preparations with the feeling of being paralyzed. Doctor Englaster seized his face and began to pinch the skin on the left side, and Harsh lost the paralysis. He knocked the rubber-covered hands away from his face and sat up.

"Get away from me, goddamn it. The operation is off."

"Indeed?"

"I've changed my mind about going through with it."

Harsh could tell nothing from their faces. The masks gave all of them the poker faces to end all poker faces.

"Will the rest of you step outside a moment?" Brother's voice was gentle. "Mr. Harsh and I will discuss this."

"Goddamn it, don't leave me in here with him!" Harsh was frightened.

No one offered to interfere. Miss Muirz, Doctor Englaster, and Mr. Hassam left the room. Brother came to the bed and looked down at Harsh. His voice was still placid. "Let me refresh your memory, Harsh."

"I know I agreed to having my face scarred, anyway I think I did. But it's off."

"Harsh, do you recall I had you investigated? The detective agency from Kansas City? Do you also recall we learned a Mr. D. C. Roebuck, a photographic supply house drummer, met violent death while pursuing you to collect an unpaid account?"

"I didn't kill the guy."

"Don't interrupt. A witness, a service station attendant, accepted a bribe to say you were not the man D. C. Roebuck pursued. I told you that. What I did not tell you is that the same witness, for the same bribe, if ordered to do so, will testify you *were* the man D. C. Roebuck pursued, and that he saw a large nickel-plated revolver in your hand. The same revolver, for your information, was found in D. C. Roebuck's wrecked car. I need not tell you how it got there."

Harsh eyed him, stunned. "What are you trying to tell me?"

"That I can have you tried and electrocuted for the murder of D. C. Roebuck just by going to a telephone."

Harsh felt sick. "You think you've got me, don't you?"

"I have got you, you idiot. You are right in my pocket where you belong, or you are right in the electric chair. That is your choice." Brother went to the door and opened it and put his head out. "Harsh has chosen to go along with us."

The time required for the operation was less than half an hour. Doctor Englaster used a local anesthetic and the most pain Harsh felt came when the needle pinked his

cheek the first time. The left side of his face became
numb, the knife did not hurt at all. Neither did the stuff
that was sprinkled in the wound before the gauze was
applied. Doctor Englaster, obviously pleased with his
own work, indicated Harsh need not necessarily stay in
bed, but he should keep the bandage in place. "You will
like that scar, Harsh. It will be quite a distinguished scar."

Harsh looked at him bitterly. "Distinguished my ass."
He pulled the liquor table to where he could reach it from
his bed and poured bourbon into a glass.

Doctor Englaster watched him with satisfaction. "Harsh,
you please me. We need a twenty-four-carat cur for this
job, and you show every sign of qualifying." He got his
instruments together and pushed the instrument table to
the door. "Miss Vera Sue Crosby has a badly bruised jaw
this morning. I treated her."

Harsh scowled at him. "I like you too, Doc." The anesthetic in the side of his face made him lisp.

Mr. Hassam began language lessons that afternoon. He
came into Harsh's room carrying a book. Mr. Hassam's
sport shirt was purple with gold flowers and his slacks
were pink linen, his sandals held to his feet by straps
between his plump toes.

"Brother sort of got the best of you, didn't he, Harsh?"

"Yeah, I guess. But my day will roll around."

"Between you and I, Harsh, I hope I am on hand that
day."

"I'll send you word."

Mr. Hassam grinned and gave Harsh the book and
asked him to read aloud from it. The book was not in
Spanish, as Harsh expected, but in English. He began to

read, but his efforts to pronounce the longer words caused Mr. Hassam's expression to grow pained. Mr. Hassam took the book back.

"The truth is my cheeks are sore from that stuff this morning, and I can't read real clear."

"The truth is you are practically illiterate, Harsh. But no matter."

"Well, I guess you might say I can't read and write real good." Harsh pointed at the book. "What's your idea trying me out on an English book?"

"I was merely ascertaining how you put printed letters into sound. We had better stick to verbal instruction and forget the books." Mr. Hassam pointed to the table. "*La mesa.*"

"Huh?"

"The Spanish word for the table. *La mesa.* Repeat after me. We will commence with the names of objects and things, then we will make them into simple sentences and go over and over them until they are fixed in your mind."

"Say, couldn't we put it off? My face hurts from that needle gunk, like I said."

"Time is of the essence."

"If that means it stinks, you're so right." Harsh lay back. "Well, shoot."

His face continued to hurt from the scar operation, and he kept thinking the last thing he felt like doing today was learn some gook language. If he didn't sort of like Mr. Hassam, he thought, he wouldn't be going along with it. "*El telefono en la mesa.*" The concentration made his head ache, and he really did not give a hoot if he never learned to say the telephone was on the table.

"Hassam, I got it figured you folks are doctoring me up to double for somebody. What I can't figure, is who."

"Good grief. Hasn't Brother told you any facts?"

"Brother tells me nothing. He hates my insides."

"Well, I'm sure you should know."

"How about telling me?"

"Telling you what?"

"Who am I going to double for?"

"Why, *El Presidente*. The president of our nation in South America."

Harsh did not say another word on the subject. He had not believed Mr. Hassam. Sons of bitches were a bunch of kidders, he decided.

THIRTEEN

The following two days were filled with a peace which puzzled Harsh. He knew that Miss Muirz, Doctor Englaster, and Mr. Hassam must have gone away, basing this conclusion on the fact that he did not see them about. No one told him whether they had departed permanently. He thought of asking Brother about it, but he decided he would not give Brother the satisfaction of saying a damn word to him. He was cultivating a murderous dislike of Brother, and along with thinking about methods of getting into the wall safe, he was letting his mind take an excursion into ways of shutting Brother up permanently.

In the meantime Mr. Hassam reached New York and made the bank deposit. He presented the card with Harsh's fingerprints along with the signature of *El Presidente* as forged by Miss Muirz. Mr. Hassam told the banker the fingerprints were part of a new policy *El Presidente* thought advisable in view of his troubled internal affairs. The thing went off with no more formality than a five-dollar savings deposit. The banker knew Mr. Hassam had been *El Presidente's* financial courier for a number of years; indeed it was Mr. Hassam who had arranged a reception with *El Presidente* and a pleasant evening when the banker was touring South America with his wife two years previously. Mr. Hassam left whistling. No more sweat than a snake swallowing eggs, he thought.

He took his customary succession of taxicabs in a zig-

zagging route uptown to a small shop on Seventh Avenue,
near Macy's. The Seventh Avenue shop was operated by a
near countryman of Mr. Hassam's, a Jordanian named
Ghaset, who carried on a small plastics manufacturing
business. The man was actually a wizard with plastics. He
could do something that, so far as Mr. Hassam knew, no
one else could or would do. He could furnish a mastic to
be applied to a human hand, peeled off when dry, and
from this he could fashion a glove which anyone with a
hand of similar size could wear to duplicate the fingerprints of the original hand. The price for this was five
thousand dollars. He and Mr. Hassam did business without delay.

Brother came in and took Harsh's temperature once each
six hours, but otherwise the two did not see each other.
During the first twenty-four hours following the scar
operation Harsh did not leave his room. He tried several
times to get into the wall safe, succeeding as usual in
opening nothing but the outer door to which he had the
combination. The only progress he was making as far as
he could see, he was getting so he could work the combination lock in nothing flat. That was something. He
wedged a match head behind the painting that covered
the safe, placing the match head in such a position that
it would drop unnoticed to the floor if the painting was
disturbed. Then he felt he could take a walk for some
much-needed exercise.

   The house seemed to be more castle than had been his
first impression, a wedding cake castle under whipped
cream clouds, the lawn tailored green velvet, each shrub
placed with landscaper's perfection. Half the jerk towns

in the country did not have a schoolhouse so large, Harsh thought. The grounds were some ten acres enclosed in a high pink coral wall on three sides. On the fourth side the wall ran into the sea and enclosed a lime-white beach where there were two thatched cabanas resembling South Sea island huts as Hollywood would conceive them.

Harsh took a stroll to the iron gate. It looked solid, but it could be unfastened from the inside with a whack from a heavy rock, if he was any judge of padlocks. But it would be noisy. On the wall, starting about as high as a man could reach by jumping and extending over the top and probably down the outside of the wall, jagged broken glass was embedded. A man might have trouble getting out of the place.

He moved on to the beach and sprawled on a deck chair in front of one of the cabanas. He wondered if he should worry about getting out of the place. The hell with being scared, he thought, let him get hold of the fifty thousand dollars and he could jump the wall flatfooted. He watched the sea. The sunlight was as warm and relaxing as soft honey poured from a pitcher. Boats moved past on a rifle blue sea. A helicopter flailed along a hundred feet overhead following the beach, and later so did a couple of light planes. The chick-like outcries of bathers came intermittently from the unseen beaches to the north and to the south, never near enough for him to distinguish what they were so happy about.

For lunch the co-pilot/servant brought a tray on which was bouillon, garlic bread, an omelet, and sweetish black coffee.

"You fly the food around too, do you, buddy?"

The man kept a wooden face. "*No habla, Señor.*" He

placed the tray on the sand beside Harsh and left. Harsh
wondered what would have happened if he had sprung
some of the Spanish he had learned on the man. What
excuses would he have had then not to strike up a conversation?

There was a telephone on a small table in the cabana.
Harsh noticed it through the cabana entrance. He stared
at the telephone for some time and abruptly got up and
went into the cabana and picked up the telephone directory on which the instrument was sitting.

If there's one in the telephone book, he thought, it'll
be in the classified section. Under L. L for Locksmith.
His hand was shaking until he had to wedge the telephone directory against the wall while he turned pages.
Security Locksmithing Company. He threw back his
head and showed all his teeth at the ceiling, wishing he
could let out a howl of satisfaction. By God, there was a
locksmith in Palm Beach. There really was.

As the fellow says, nothing gets results like action, he
reflected, and he picked up the telephone.

"May I serve you?"

It was Brother's voice.

Harsh froze. He had made a mistake here, he had
made a real mistake. The damn line plugged into a private switchboard at the house, and Brother had been
keeping an eye on it. What could he do about it? He did
not want Brother to know he had even toyed with the
idea of using the telephone. He held his breath, wondering whether he had gasped or anything earlier so that
he could have been heard. Jesus, if he put the telephone

back on the cradle now, Brother would know for sure something was screwy.

His eyes chanced on the luncheon tray sitting on the sand outside. I need a table to eat my lunch off of, don't I? he thought. As quietly as he could he placed the telephone on the cabana floor where it might have fallen if dislodged from the table. Then he picked up the telephone table one-handed, carried it outside, and plunked the legs down in the sand beside his chair. He maneuvered the luncheon tray onto the table, bracing it against his cast. Then he sat down and picked up knife and fork. He ate two bites before Brother came running from the direction of the house.

Brother looked into the cabana. "That telephone is off its hook."

"It is? Say, I guess it fell off the table when I moved the thing out here. Put it back, will you? If I bend over to do anything, this face of mine stabs me blind."

Brother's syrup-dipped eyes stayed on Harsh. His lips were compressed. His breath came and went through his nose rather audibly. Then Brother began to call Harsh things in Spanish, words too fast for Harsh to understand, but which had the tongue lash that profanity has in any language.

Harsh waved a forkful of food at Brother. "Cuss all you want to, you crazy bastard. You think I care?"

Brother became suddenly pale and silent. Then he wheeled and strode back to the house and went inside. Harsh was both surprised and amused, and he was congratulating himself on having gotten rid of the man when Brother reappeared from the house. Now Brother had a shotgun. He came back to the cabana at a run.

Harsh got wildly to his feet, not knowing what he was going to do, feeling sure Brother was going to shoot him down. His skin felt like it was crawling with lice, so great was his nervous tension. Brother ran straight to him and jammed the muzzle of the shotgun against his chest. It was a double-barreled shotgun, a hammer model, and Harsh could see it was cocked. All right, I am going to die anyway, what is there to lose, Harsh thought. He fell back on his army training. It was no trick, the instructor had told them, to disarm a man who has a gun on you providing the gun is jammed against your body. You just grab the gun and knock it aside. It is a matter of the telegraphic speed of nerve impulses. If the gun is jammed against some part of your torso, you can make it, because it takes a split second for your brain to send the grab message to your muscles, and a split second for the other man's brain to send the message that you are going to grab, pull the trigger. Your message gets the first start, and this is the difference. Enough difference.

Harsh was twisting when he struck the gun. It went off. Noise, a tubful of fire, powder stink. A hole appeared in the sand at their feet large enough to be a grave for a small pig. Jesus God, Harsh thought, it worked, that hairy-chested instructor wasn't fly-specking us. Harsh got his usable arm over the barrel of the shotgun and spun his body completely around and the shotgun was torn from Brother's grip. The gun sailed about twenty feet, landing in the foam where a wave was falling apart on the sand. Now Brother stood spraddle-legged and wide open for a kick, so Harsh let him have it. In the groin.

Brother fell backward when the kick got him, but instead of turning green and staying down, he got up again at once. Harsh ran for the shotgun. He tripped and fell face first into the wet sand, but got his good hand on the shotgun after what seemed forever, and sat up. A wave came in and broke and drenched him with salt water almost to the hip pockets. He watched Brother. "You want the other barrel?"

"Give me that gun, Harsh."

"I'll give you what's in the barrel, I ain't kidding you."

There was a silence—what the fellow would call a pregnant silence, Harsh thought. He glowered over the shotgun sights and kept the muzzle pointed at Brother's face.

Brother smiled a rather odd smile. If the smile was intended to worry Harsh, it succeeded, for he felt certain Brother was going to come at him again. But Brother turned and walked, in no hurry at all, back to the house.

Harsh tried to get up from the wet sand, but his legs refused the job. He looked down at the shotgun, and then he realized—he was sure by looking at the down hammers—that both barrels had exploded when Brother fired the gun. He had been threatening Brother with an empty weapon.

FOURTEEN

When Harsh saw Mr. Hassam the next morning, he threw up his arm and waved him over. He was very glad to see him. Mr. Hassam walked into the sun-splashed dining patio adjacent to the kitchen where Harsh was sitting on an iron spider chair eating breakfast. "You got back, eh? It seemed like you were gone forever."

"I came in this morning early." Mr. Hassam waved at the table. "I like to get my own breakfast. Excuse me." He went into the kitchen.

Harsh listened to pans rattling for a time, then moved over to the kitchen door. "What are you fixing yourself?"

"Pompano sautéed in butter with capers. I like fish for breakfast. Could I fix you some?"

"I guess I could go for a little more. I got an appetite this morning, for a change. I'm glad to see you back, Mr. Hassam. I mean that. Nobody else around here offers to prepare me breakfast."

"Thank you, Harsh. I do not see why you should not be popular."

"Neither do I, but I keep having run-ins with different people around here."

"You mean Brother?"

Harsh nodded. "Yeah, that's who I mean. You know something, I never seen a guy like that bastard. I mean I don't make him out. No crap. He scares the hell out of me, I'm not fooling you. You know what he tried to do yesterday afternoon? Blow my gut right out of me with a shotgun. Blow it right out of me."

Mr. Hassam poured coffee into a cup. "Yes. Brother told me this morning. He is very sorry. He said he lost his head. He asked me to express his regrets."

"He what?"

"He is very sorry, and wants to express his regrets."

Harsh laughed. "Do you expect me to believe that?"

"Harsh, I could explain how you can avoid future trouble with Brother. I mean, I can tell you some things that may help you exercise restraint and tolerance."

"I'll restrain him with a brickbat, he points that shotgun at me again."

"Harsh, here is the first thing I want to tell you. Brother has a mental handicap, an affliction known as paranoia. It comes and goes, and sometimes it reaches the point where he has to go to a sanitarium and take shock treatments."

"That's no news to me, Mr. Hassam. I had figured out he was nuts. You just watch him, anybody would know."

"Harsh, if you will make allowances for his illness, I think you can handle him. Particularly now, since you bested him in the encounter yesterday."

"Oh, he figured I licked him, did he? He had me guessing. I couldn't tell what he thought. He ruined my night's sleep. I kept wondering when he was going to pop in on me with another shotgun. That's a tough boy, that Brother. You know what I did, I kicked him right in the privates as hard as I could. It didn't faze the bastard. He got up ready to eat me. And he would have, except by then I had my mitts on the blunderbuss."

"That is not so strange."

"Listen, a kick in the testes like that would put me down for good."

"Not if you didn't have them."

Harsh's jaw dropped. "The hell you say! Is that what he is? I thought those guys were soft and peaceful."

"Well, Brother is not. Brother adheres to a routine of rigorous diet and exercise, perhaps to subdue evidence of his handicap, I don't know."

"I'm glad you told me about it, Mr. Hassam. Nobody tells me anything but you. I feel kind of sorry for the guy, at that."

"Yes, and you would feel even sorrier if I told you who did it to him."

"I would? Why?"

"It was his brother."

"Jesus. You mean his own brother—Jesus!"

Mr. Hassam tasted of a caper. "*El Presidente*."

Harsh stared. "You mean *El Presidente* is his...and he had him *castrated*? The guy I look like?"

"Now you're getting it."

"Jesus. The first time Brother laid eyes on me, back in that hospital, he gave one hell of a jump. He hated me right off, and he's hated me ever after. I can begin to see why."

Mr. Hassam transferred pompano to plates with the skill of a chef. "I trust this information will enable you to be more tolerant."

"Yeah, it will make his crap easier to swallow." Harsh accepted one of the plates. "What was the trouble between the brothers, anyway?"

Mr. Hassam smiled thinly. "Miss Muirz. They had a falling out over her."

Harsh put the plate holding the pompano on the kitchen cabinet. He stood there for a while. "Miss Muirz." He picked up a cup of coffee and drank it all. "Well, it figures."

Harsh had intended to bring up the subject of the fingerprints on the bank deposit card but the news about Brother caused him to forget it until after breakfast, when Mr. Hassam brought out the mastic material he had brought with him from New York for the hand casts. The materials consisted of a little tin spray can and a jar of the mastic itself which was the color of taffy candy before it is pulled. Harsh was puzzled, but he followed instructions and sat down and permitted his hands to be sprayed from the can—both hands, the healthy one and the one in the cast. This placed an oily coating on his skin, designed to keep the mastic from adhering to the skin.

Harsh watched Mr. Hassam open the jar of mastic. "Hey, wait a minute. What is this for?"

"You need not be afraid."

"I ain't worried about my yellow feathers. What is that gunk, is what I wanta know."

"We are going to have a custom-made pair of gloves fashioned for you, Harsh."

"Yeah? Is that right, now?" Harsh drew his hands back. "Just a new pair of gloves, huh?"

"You're not scared, are you?"

"You know how it is. You're sure you're being framed, you get shotguns pointed at your belly, and you get cute answers to questions. I ain't scared, but I get to wondering."

"I wish you would go along with me, Harsh." Mr. Hassam sounded tired. "I have to do this. I have to get these gloves made, gloves which will carry your fingerprints, so that we can place your prints on additional bank deposit cards. You can understand, we can't run all the way up here from South America with every bank deposit card. That is all there is to it."

"Hell, I thought maybe you were going to knock off some guy and leave my prints on the job."

"No, no, nothing like that. I swear it."

"I think you're nuts, Mr. Hassam, no crap. I never ran across such a wild scheme before."

"Trust me, Harsh."

"Well, okay." Harsh held out his right hand. "I guess I got very little choice."

When Mr. Hassam had stripped the set-up mastic off Harsh's hands, he left the kitchen at once with it, leaving Harsh to do some second-thinking. He immediately wished he had not consented to having the hand casts made. Why had he been such a sucker, anyway? Mr. Hassam was a slick one, talking him into it. If they were going to make some gloves that anybody could wear and leave his fingerprints scattered around, that was serious. They could rob Fort Knox if they could figure out a way to get the job done, and hang it on him if they wanted to.

He felt something wriggling down his forehead. He struck it a hard blow with his palm, but it was just a drop of sweat, which he splashed to nothing.

He went over to the kitchen sink and washed the oily film off his hands, taking care not to get the cast wet. He had to use quite a lot of soap powder to get it off. Then he examined the gunk still left in the jar. There was not much of it. No label on the jar, no way to tell who made the stuff. Well, he had made another sucker move, that was what he had done.

He looked at Mr. Hassam narrowly when the latter rejoined him almost two hours later. "Them things you made of my hands, were they all right? They satisfy you?"

"Perfectly."

"Could I have a look at them? I'd kinda like to see what they look like." If he got his hands on the casts, he was going to destroy them.

"I'm sorry, Harsh. I have already sent them off to New York by air mail."

"Oh." Harsh rubbed the side of his nose with his finger. "Well, I guess that's that. What else is on the toboggan for today?"

"More Spanish lessons, if you feel up to it."

"Why not."

"Shall we go down to the beach, then? More comfortable there."

The sea with the early morning sun falling across it looked licorice black, with swatches of scintillating brilliance following along on the wave crests.

"Not that you ain't good company, but I would rather sit on the beach with Miss Muirz, if you know what I mean." Harsh took off his shoes and socks and dug his bare feet into the warm sand. "What happened to that dish anyway?"

"She had a business trip to make. I imagine she may return today."

"Yeah?" Harsh grinned. "I hardly got to know her, she

was in and out of here like the Irishman's flea. So she's gonna be back, huh? Well, that should pick up things around here."

Mr. Hassam looked at him with amusement. "You have my felicitations."

Harsh eyed him. "Yeah. What in the hell's a felicitation?"

"A blessing."

"Yeah. You mean with your fingers crossed, the way you sound."

A wave came swelling in and fell on the ash blond beach at their feet with an audible grunt. Mr. Hassam kicked some dry sand out of the wet sand. "Maybe we should get at the Spanish lesson."

"If you say so."

"How much do you remember of what we have already gone over, Harsh?"

For some time they practiced what Mr. Hassam called the lilt of the Spanish tongue, which Harsh decided was mostly a way of pronouncing each vowel with great clarity as if he was attacking the sound. He learned how to take the fuzzy edges off his vowels, and how to put vowel glides in certain places so as to lay a special emphasis. A lot of noodle soup, Harsh thought, but he kept at it.

"You are progressing excellently, Mr. Harsh."

"Yeah. Well you would have a time proving it by me. This stuff is way out of my line. Say, am I supposed to be able to spout this stuff like a native? I'll never make it."

"A smattering will do."

"Maybe this *El Presidente* made some speeches or something, ones that were recorded, that I could listen to. Wouldn't that help?"

"That will come later."

"Okay."

They watched a small plane come down the shoreline. The plane had its nose down to within fifty feet of the surf and was making time down the beach. The pilot waved when he went past. Harsh waved back. "That's a lucky bastard, that pilot. You know I always wished I could fly one of them things. Lot of 'em by here. Must be twenty, thirty, a day. Lot of sightseeing."

"Tourists, I imagine." Mr. Hassam was not much interested in the plane.

"Yeah, I suppose. A treat for them poor tourists, I bet, getting a look at a palace like this. It ain't every day you see something that fancy." The plane had passed on, dragging a broom of sound over the beach. "Take my old man, he wouldn't believe this. He was a farmer. He had his feet in the clay all his life. He never knew he was sweating his guts out so some people could live high on the hog in places like this. I wonder what he would have thought, give him a look at this." Harsh glanced at Mr. Hassam. "Maybe it ain't nothing unusual to you, though."

Mr. Hassam looked sober. "I, too, had a humble beginning." He lay back on the sand and began to talk. He said Harsh might not believe it, but this was a far cry from his own youth also. All but the sand. The sand was the same. Sand was sand, and Mr. Hassam's had been in dunes, hot as a furnace by day and as nice as a woman at night. "Mr. Harsh, I was born on the sand in a rug tent, begat by a father who bred white asses of fine quality which he exported to Mecca. He bought my mother in a market for a sum of silver piastres the equal of about twenty-five dollars American. Mr. Harsh, does that sound romantic, picturesque? It was not, believe me. I cannot remember a time when I was not hungry there in that desert, and you should have seen me, a skinny teenage kid riding a white ass or a camel. I was seventeen when my father sent me to sell a herd of the asses to a Mecca dealer, and do you know what I did? I took the money the dealer paid and I never went back. I have not seen my father nor my mother again until this day. I went to Damascus, became a fat boy in Damascus. You know what is a fat boy in Damascus? No, nothing nasty. Just a boy the desert has given a permanent hunger for food. I went to work for an importer. In time I found the importer was doing a smuggling business and paying off the local police and bigwigs with a bag of Dutch gold once a month, a bag of gulden left discreetly at the house of the girlfriend of an official. That Dutch gold intrigued me. For decades Dutch gulden have been the most dependable of the world currencies. Anyway, I befriended the girl, we tipped off the military, and we came out of it with one bag of Dutch gold. Or rather, I did, because I left the girl behind but not the gold, and went to Cairo for schooling, and then to Oxford, a great university in England, and then to South America to be a college professor with a specialty in finance. So you see, Mr. Harsh, one thing leads to another and here we are."

Mr. Hassam fell silent and his eyes were shiny with memories.

Harsh waggled his toes in the sand and scratched his face around the edge of the bandage and wondered what was the pitch. He could not think of anything that could have put Mr. Hassam in a reminiscing mood. They had not been drinking or anything. The fat little slicker is leading up to something, Harsh decided.

"Yeah, Mr. Hassam, here we are."

"Two men perhaps more alike in environmental molding than you at first presumed, eh, Mr. Harsh? Two men with the same greed and the same needs."

Harsh watched a wave march up the beach. "So you figure I'm greedy?"

"Well, are you not?"

"Sure. I guess so. Who ain't? When you come right down to it, who ain't?"

"No one, I imagine."

Harsh dumped sand out of one of his shoes.

"I don't mind talking to you, Mr. Hassam. You're a very interesting talker. But ain't you afraid of wearing the bush out by beating around it? What I mean, why not come to the point?"

Mr. Hassam's eyes were suddenly alert and shiny. "I was coming to the point."

"Yeah? How, by way of Detroit and points between? What are you driving at anyway?"

"Harsh, I was pointing out that we both like money."

"Well goddamn it now, I know what you were pointing out. I understand the word money."

"Harsh, you had a narrow escape yesterday. With the telephone in the cabana, I mean."

"I wouldn't know what you mean. And if I did, I would have a hell of a time figuring out what it had to do with money. I'm sorry, I don't follow you, Mr. Hassam."

"Harsh, you did not knock that telephone off the table

accidentally. What you did, you picked up the telephone to make an outside call. Possibly you planned to reach a confederate to help you crack this nut. You found the telephone was not an outside line, and Brother answered on the switchboard, so you pretended the phone had just been knocked off the table. That was quick thinking, Harsh. A man who was not alert, a man who did not have natural instincts of wariness, would have hung up the phone. That is what a stupid man would have done. But you did not. You were a wary man."

Harsh watched the other intently. "Mr. Hassam, I don't know what you're driving at. You've got me going."

"I am trying to tell you the telephone incident convinced me you are the kind of a man it would be safe to do business with, Harsh."

"How was that?"

"You can think on your feet. I mean thinking on your feet comes naturally to you."

"I guess opinions about that might differ."

Mr. Hassam gave the neighborhood a precautionary look. "You do not need to call in an outside confederate, Harsh. Not when you have one ready-made who knows the ropes."

"I guess you mean you and I might work something together."

"Precisely."

"We put out heads together, is that it?"

"Yes."

"You help me, I help you. That the idea?"

"Yes."

"Mr. Hassam, how do you expect me to help you? I mean, what will I have to do?"

Mr. Hassam smiled thinly. "That will come. I am sure it will come. Frankly, I had not yet worked out a plan."

"Well, you can help me right now. I already got my problem. My problem is fifty thousand dollars in that safe, plus nineteen hundred for my car. That son of a bitching Brother locked the money in the safe and gave me one key and kept the other key himself. My problem is to get my dough out of that safe."

"Yes, I know about that."

"There by God is one place you can help me right now."

Mr. Hassam tilted his head back and watched an airplane that was circling high in the sky above the sea. "I do not have the other key to the safe, you know." The plane's wings gave off reflections of light like faint sparks.

"Well, I know one way to get the key off Brother. Knock the son of a bitch on the head and take it."

"Yes. Yes indeed." Mr. Hassam's voice was dry. "Then you could pocket the fifty thousand, and off you could go. Right?"

Harsh's eyes narrowed. "I get it."

"You get what?"

"You wouldn't just hand me the fifty thousand bucks now, would you. I mean, that would be a real sucker deal for you."

Mr. Hassam nodded. "I think we are beginning to reach a sense of compatibility."

"You could call it that, I suppose." Harsh caught a movement near the house. "Look, Hassam, this sniffing around the post you're doing, are you figuring you might latch onto a part of my fifty thousand?"

Hassam smiled. "Not in the least. I might even add to it, if things break right."

The figure at the house was Brother, who had popped into view and was running toward them. "We better knock it off. Here comes Brother."

"Where?" Mr. Hassam looked around.

Harsh pointed. "He's got the ants for some reason. Look at him run."

Brother ran toward them with the long loping lurching pace of a distance man. He had been interrupted while shaving for there was lather on one side of his face and he carried a towel in one hand.

Brother confronted Mr. Hassam breathlessly. "Miss Muirz. Long distance. Urgent. You are to return at once. I looked all over hell for you."

"We were here on the beach, working on his Spanish." Mr. Hassam's face began to be less coffee-colored. "Urgent, you say? Has something gone wrong?"

Brother drew himself erect. "*El Presidente* has resigned."

Mr. Hassam turned and ran toward the house.

PART THREE

FIFTEEN

El Presidente had made his move against the Catholics, and it had not worked out as he had hoped. Posturing, shouting, standing on the balcony of the Presidential residence on *Avenida del Libertador General San Martin*— he had learned the effectiveness of the balcony speech from Mussolini a long time ago—he made his bluff, screaming that he would resign his office if the people wished, if the people felt it would bring peace and prosperity. The expected cries thundered back from the mob below. *No, no! Prefero El Presidente! Viva la Señora de la Esperanza!* However the crowd had amounted to only about thirty thousand, which was disappointing, since the organizers of the *descamisada*, the shirtless ones, had worked like dogs and had been able to turn out but little more than half of the fifty thousand demanded of them. Also the wave of hysteria that swept the shirtless ones was neither violent nor long-lived.

The moment he got back from Miami, Mr. Hassam could sense a change in the people. He went to the bank at once. Not officially an officer of the bank, he had however access to its information pipelines, and the conclusion he drew was that the inevitable had come. He heard that two Catholic leaders, two prominent Bishops, had been tossed in jail accused of sex perversion. Mr. Hassam felt the bastard had made a real big mistake there. Rumors were tearing like sky rockets through the town, the main

one a report that some of the army leaders had been
unable to stomach the rank thing with the Catholic prel-
ates, and had set up a clique among themselves.

Mr. Hassam had as yet found no reliable evidence that
El Presidente had resigned. He wondered if the bastard
was shacked up somewhere with one of his tarts and
doing nothing about the situation, happy to fiddle while
Rome burned. Mr. Hassam was fairly sure he had resigned, however, or was resigning—Miss Muirz had said
so, and Miss Muirz was the one person *El Presidente* was
likely to confide in.

The telephone rang in Mr. Hassam's office and he
jumped like a gazelle.

"My place. Right away. You took your time getting
down here."

Miss Muirz's voice.

"On my way. Did my best." Nervousness made Mr.
Hassam just as cryptic as she.

Miss Muirz lived in a four-story house in *Calle Cor-
rientes*, and this was Mr. Hassam's first visit to the house.
He expected to be impressed and he was; the luxury, the
costliness of the furnishings, struck him as fantastic. Also
the taste was far worse than he expected, so bad that he
wondered if she had gone back to sleeping with *El
Presidente*, although the way the grapevine had it, for
two years this had not been the case. The garish display
of gold bric-a-brac, tapestries and old masters was exactly
the kind of rich foulness that appealed to *El Presidente*.
Or maybe, Mr. Hassam reflected, Miss Muirz was keeping
the awful decorative scheme intact as a shrine to her
memories, in which case *El Presidente* must have been a
better lover than anyone thought.

Doctor Englaster arrived shortly and was let in by the same unspeaking, dour-faced servant who had admitted Mr. Hassam. Miss Muirz had still not made an appearance. "Good afternoon, Achmed. You got the call also, did you?"

Mr. Hassam did not like to be called Achmed. It was his given name and it was also the name under which he had once been sent to prison. "Is it true, Doctor?"

"I am not sure. Rumors. Rumors everywhere, like buzzing hornets. Have you any facts?"

"I have seen no one who is on the inside." Mr. Hassam waved a hand at the room they stood in. "I am surprised she has not loaded up a lot of this crap and dumped it in the river. I would if it was me."

"The place is a bit of a circus ring, all right." Doctor Englaster had found a cabinet which turned into a bar when one lifted the top. "I see we have potables here. What do you say we place a cushion, liquid form, under the shock I suspect we are in for."

Before they could mix drinks, Miss Muirz appeared in the doorway. "I was on the telephone." She poured the liquor for them. "Gentlemen, I offer you a toast." She raised her glass to the level of her eyes. "A toast to the great and illustrious leader of our nation, the accumulator of certain funds cached abroad, who is on his way out. In other words, I had a talk with *El Presidente* this morning."

Doctor Englaster nodded. "How did you catch his attention, disguise yourself as a high-school student?"

Mr. Hassam kept all expression off his face, but he wished he had said that to her, he wished he had had the guts. He did not like her. He did not like her smug way of knowing everything before anyone else knew it, which was her specialty. Also he did not like Doctor Englaster.

Miss Muirz sank lazily onto a chair. "Thank you, Doctor. You make it easier for me to spoil your day. As I have it, he has resigned."

Mr. Hassam moistened his lips with the tip of his tongue. "But news like that is not out anywhere."

"I don't think he has resigned." Doctor Englaster made liquor swirl around and around in his glass. "He lacks that much sense. What do you say, Achmed, does he have that much sense left?"

"Good God!" Mr. Hassam was feeling weak. "We do not have Harsh ready to take his place."

"He has resigned." Miss Muirz did not blink her eyes. "He told me so himself. This morning."

"Goddamn!" Doctor Englaster began to look as if someone had shut off his wind. "You mean this is not a joke?"

Mr. Hassam looked at Doctor Englaster in surprise, realizing for the first time that the Doctor had been treating the whole thing as a joke because he actually thought it was one. Why, the overbearing fool, Mr. Hassam thought. How could he be so stupid?

"The clique who ousted him is keeping it quiet until they have full control over the government." Miss Muirz was almost too calm to suit Mr. Hassam. "*El Presidente* is in hiding."

Mr. Hassam put his glass down quickly. "You talked to him?"

"Yes."

"In person?"

"Yes, this morning. This afternoon again, by telephone."

"Where is he hiding?"

"I do not know."

"But if you talked to him in person…"

"That was at the palace, before he resigned. He had his resignation in his hand, carrying it around with him as if it was a monstrous thing. The way he looked at the paper. I felt so sorry for him."

"But where is he hiding now?"

"I do not know."

"The situation is serious, anyway." Mr. Hassam was watching Miss Muirz closely, for he was becoming puzzled by her calmness, or rather her appearance of calmness. He suddenly decided she was not calm at all. She was rigid with tension, that was what she was. She was far more affected than any of them.

Doctor Englaster gestured jerkily. "What is that rat bastard planning to do? Throw us out in the cold?" His right hand was wet with spilled liquor.

Miss Muirz's eyes were strangely blank. "Doctor, you are spilling your liquor."

"That dirty double-crossing rat." Doctor Englaster clenched a fist. "He could not have put off going into exile until we were safely ready to kill the son of a bitch and put Harsh in his shoes."

Mr. Hassam was watching Miss Muirz at the moment, and he learned something. When Doctor Hassam mentioned murdering *El Presidente*, there were signs of a suppressed inner convulsion apparent with Miss Muirz. Mr. Hassam was shocked. Good God, she still loves the scoundrel, he thought.

Miss Muirz addressed Doctor Englaster quietly. "Stop howling childlike remarks, Doctor. I called you two gentlemen here to tell you why *El Presidente* telephoned me. This is the reason. He wants us to take his personal possessions out of the country."

Mr. Hassam was not deceived by her quiet voice. Inside she was very tense. When it comes time to kill *El Presidente*, Mr. Hassam reflected, we must arrange it so she is not in the vicinity and better still does not know about it until the slaying is an accomplished fact. He did not trust women with the temperament of Miss Muirz to withstand emotional shock in any predictable fashion.

"What property?" Mr. Hassam showed interest.

"Paintings and his late wife's jewelry."

Mr. Hassam nodded, for the oil paintings were very desirable items, several having been purchased from the late Hermann Goering collection at the time the Third Reich was a going concern and in need of *El Presidente's* friendship, and bought at a terrific bargain, while the jewelry had been accumulated by *El Presidente's* late wife prior to her death, and it too was fabulous for she had felt compelled to outdo all the family jewels in the nation.

Mr. Hassam smiled. "Good. If he wants us to get the personal stuff out for him, it shows he intends to join us later."

Doctor Englaster groaned. "Goddamn paintings and goddamn jewelry, chicken feed."

Mr. Hassam glanced at him. "He paid two million for the paintings. She paid five times that for the jewelry. I happen to know the appraisal six months ago was nearly seventeen million. What chicken did you have in mind feeding, Doctor?"

Doctor Englaster belched. Mr. Hassam abruptly realized he was somewhat intoxicated.

"The oil paintings, the jewelry, will they be difficult to assemble?" Mr. Hassam looked inquiringly at Miss Muirz.

"No trouble. Actually it is all in a room in this house right now. *El Presidente* himself brought it here."

Mr. Hassam went to the portable bar and began mixing another round of drinks. So that was what had gotten her worked up; the old lover had come running to her in his moment of need, arousing her mother complex or something. He wondered what would be aroused when they actually got ready to assassinate *El Presidente*. Suddenly he suppressed a shudder.

"I can supply transportation."

"Very good, Mr. Hassam."

"Where is *El Presidente* now?"

"I do not know. I told you that."

"Oh, yes." Mr. Hassam doubled the amount of liquor in each glass in the drinks he was making. "He may lie low. That would be the sensible procedure, go into sanctuary until the storm subsides." He noticed that his own hand was shaking. "They will clamor for his blood, and he will know that."

"Where would the rat hide?" Doctor Englaster's voice was fuzzy.

"Well, there are the traditional sanctuaries, the monasteries and churches." Miss Muirz accepted a drink with a hand which was very pale but also very steady. "However, there is also a Uruguayan gunboat in the harbor and *El Presidente* may seek sanctuary aboard her. He would be safest there. A mob might storm a church, or soldiers also. But a gunboat is diplomatically the home soil of its own nation, and no mob is going to tackle a gunboat, nor soldiers either."

"Jesus! That is where he is now, then!" Doctor Englaster jerkily wiped his palms on a handkerchief. "Give me one of those drinks, Hassam. God, I need it. I was half drunk when I came over here, feeling something like this was going to fall on us."

Mr. Hassam handed him one drink. "I suggest we get busy. I have a standby plane for an emergency, one I never use, and which nobody is aware I own."

Doctor Englaster spilled some liquor on his chin. "How long do you think we have?"

Miss Muirz replied with the same unalterable calmness that was like an over-stretched still wire. "I doubt *El Presidente* can leave hiding in under two weeks. Particularly if he is aboard the Uruguayan gunboat, which I expect he is, it will require two weeks to unwind the diplomatic red tape surrounding such a thing."

Mr. Hassam took a deep breath. "We may be able to get our plan in shape in two weeks."

"I predict we have two weeks." Miss Muirz's breathing was very deep and regular. Too deep and regular, Mr. Hassam felt.

"God!" Doctor Englaster gulped down the last of his drink. "Why couldn't the son of a bitch have waited a while to resign? He never did a decent thing for anybody in his whole life."

SIXTEEN

On the morning of the third day after Mr. Hassam had
departed in such haste for South America, Walter Harsh
was awakened by someone banging on his bedroom
door. The sun was not up and the room was in pale darkness. Harsh switched on the light and looked at the door
to see if the two chairs he had wedged there were still in
place. He had formed a habit of wedging chairs against
the door when he retired in order to keep out anyone
inclined to visit him while he was asleep, anyone who
might be after the wall safe key. The knocking came
from the door again. Harsh rolled out of bed, crossed
silently to the wall safe, rested his cheek on the wall to
get an eye as close to the surface as possible, and
squinted to see if the match head was still in place
between the oil painting and the wall. It was. The fist
hammered the door. Harsh turned. "Who is it? What
the hell, it's the middle of the night!"

"It's nearly daylight. Rise and shine, boy." It was Mr.
Hassam's voice.

Harsh removed the chairs and opened the door. "Hiya,
Hassam. You sure came back full of bubbles. Trip must
have agreed with you."

There were dark fatigue circles under Mr. Hassam's
eyes.

"You been running into a little trouble, Mr. Hassam?"

"Well, Harsh, we do not really know how serious it is. We cannot tell. But it is trouble, yes."

"Is there anything I can do to help you out, Mr. Hassam?"

"Yes, there is, Harsh. You see, we do not have as much time as we thought we would have. I was wondering if you would mind helping speed it up?"

"I don't mind anything reasonable. What did you have in mind?"

"If you will work very hard, Harsh, I can cram the necessary Spanish into you in a few days, I believe. Would you try it with me?"

"Sure, why not? Anything to break the monotony around here. You know it's kind of dull, with Vera Sue down on me, the servants afraid to talk to me, and me afraid to talk to Brother."

"I'm sure you can do it, Harsh."

"Like I say, anything for a change. All I been able to find to do is sit on the beach and watch the airplanes go past overhead and the boats fool around on the ocean."

Mr. Hassam glanced at his watch. "Let's go down to breakfast. The morning news will be on the radio in a few minutes. I want you to listen to it with me."

"Yeah? Something special on the radio?"

"There might be."

They had breakfast on the dining terrace. It consisted of ham prepared with maple syrup and sausages so highly spiced they made Harsh's tongue tingle. Mr. Hassam sent the servant for a radio and had it plugged in and placed on the table at his elbow. Mr. Hassam tuned in a station where the weather was on.

Harsh listened to the exaggerated version of the northern weather the Florida station was giving. Sleet, ice, snow, blizzards in New York, blizzards in Buffalo, worst cold wave of the year in Boston, St. Louis, and Los Angeles. Two deaths from freezing in Alturas, California.

"Hey, did you hear that, Hassam? In California—"

Mr. Hassam lifted a finger for silence.

The regular newscast had begun. They'd missed the beginning.

"—*throughout South America today is one of tight lips and mystery, but there is no doubt of it, the most controversial political figure of the hemisphere has fallen. Known by his people as* El Presidente, *the dictator is believed to have fled for safety to a Uruguayan gunboat now at anchor in the harbor of the capitol he has ruled with an iron hand—many say a corrupt hand —for two decades. A provisionary government guided by a junta of the military has taken over. Censorship is limiting all news, but the pattern of events is clear. If* El Presidente *is on the gunboat, as rumor has it, his enemies will surely demand that he be turned over to them for trial. Representatives of the Uruguayan government have so far refused to comment on the matter, but if the history of close relations between the countries' leaders is a guide, any demand to turn over the man under their protection will be refused. Predictions are that the gunboat will remain in harbor for as much as two weeks while diplomatic discussions are pursued, but sources say* El Presidente *is as safe within its bulkhead as he would be in a foreign country. As one former government official told us earlier this morning, 'El Presidente has always been a man who could look after his own welfare.'* "

Harsh watched Mr. Hassam take in a deep breath and let it out. "Well, Hassam? Is it bad news or good news?"

"If we could be sure he is on that gunboat, it would be just fair news."

"He is on the gunboat, Mr. Hassam. The man just said he was."

"He said it was rumored that he was. It does not mean a thing."

"They sounded pretty certain to me."

"Well, I do hope you are right."

"Where do you think he might be, if he ain't on the gunboat?"

"I wish I knew. Your guess would be as good as mine, Harsh. He is a clever devil, in spite of the mess he is in now. He might be anywhere, Switzerland, Spain, Panama. He might be right here in Florida keeping his eye on us."

"Yeah? Watching us, huh? Why would he do that?"

"*El Presidente* has hidden a sizeable fortune in various foreign countries. We did the hiding for him, Harsh. We and *El Presidente* are the only ones who know where the money is. At a time like this, he might feel it well to watch us."

"Yeah. I guess that's what I would do if I was in his shoes, if I had been sucker enough to trust you people in the first place."

Mr. Hassam smiled without much humor. "We spent years on it, Harsh. Building his confidence in us. Years, during which we never swindled him out of a cent."

"I figured you had done something like that."

"The reason I wanted you to hear the broadcast, Harsh, I wanted you to know we have no more than two weeks— if we even have that long."

"Sure, I see that."

"In no more than two weeks, you have to look, speak, think, act like *El Presidente*. You have to be him."

"I see that, too."

"Good."

"There is one thing nobody has said much about." Harsh cleared his throat. "I take it this *El Presidente* is not going to just step aside and let me masquerade as him. Okay, what makes him do it? What happens to him, and who makes it happen?"

"We will take care of that, Harsh. No need to worry."

"I don't know about that. It gives me the creeps, the way you people treat killing that guy like it was nothing. To say nothing of the way you casually mention a million bucks, just like it was an itch on the end of your nose or something."

"Don't bother yourself." Mr. Hassam patted the air in front of him with both hands. "The way we will handle it, no one will ever know anyone was killed."

"And I'll tell you something else gives me the willies, Mr. Hassam. I think you've got people mixed up in this you can't depend on in a squeeze. That Brother, that one is bugs. And Doc Englaster, going around with his nose in the air, I don't think I would depend on him in a pinch either. You pile murder on that, and it gives me the plain goddamn creeps."

Mr. Hassam leaned back and his face was wooden. "Cold feet, Harsh?"

"I'm just telling you."

"Yes, I see."

"And another goddamn thing is that fifty thousand dollars of mine, Mr. Hassam. I tell you flat, I don't get that dough, there is going to be hell to pay."

"You will get it."

"I want it now."

Mr. Hassam moved his hands wearily. "Impossible. No point in kidding around about that, Harsh, you get paid when you deliver."

"In other words, you trust the hell out of me."

"We trust you just as much as you trust us."

"Yeah?"

"Isn't that right?"

"I guess it is."

The other three conspirators appeared for breakfast. Miss Muirz, Doctor Englaster, and Brother together. Doctor Englaster's voice was shrill with excitement. "Did you hear the news on the radio, Achmed?" He had been drinking again. "I knew the bastard was on the gunboat. I knew it!"

The news broadcast on the radio had a strong effect on Harsh. It added another subject to the two about which he had been doing most of his thinking: the fifty thousand dollars and Miss Muirz. Now he was for the first time really convinced he was being groomed to be a double for a South American ex-president.

Harsh presumed there were similar news broadcasts of the event taking place throughout the country. On the Florida station, he thought, they had put it right after the weather, so that made it of prime prominence. It was an important piece of news. He was alarmed that it should be so prominent.

If it ever got out he was masquerading as that guy, Harsh thought, there would be a stink.

He tried to weigh some of the effects of such a thing by imagining he was taking the place of the President of the United States, but the idea was so preposterous he could not get any value out of the thought. But there would sure be a mess stirred up.

The thing he ought to do, Harsh decided, was haul ass out of here. It was getting about that time. Fifty thousand dollars or no fifty thousand dollars, he should get long gone from here.

It was a good sensible idea and he knew nothing would come of it because it was physically impossible for him to leave without that money. If he tried to make his legs take him away, he hoped his legs would have sense enough to drop off his body.

Walter Harsh was walking around the grounds trying to think of a way into the wall safe when he heard swishing and cracking and thudding sounds, then saw Miss Muirz. A day or two ago he had noticed there was a smooth panel insert in the wall on the north side of the grounds. The panel was several feet high and more than twenty feet wide, smooth and made of concrete. Miss Muirz had a long curved wicker basket strapped to one hand and was firing a ball at the wall and catching it on the rebound, using the basket. The ball traveled like a rifle bullet, and sounded like one whenever it hit the wall. It was almost too fast for the eye.

Miss Muirz was wearing tennis shoes, shorts, bra. She was trim and very athletic. She was about the best looking thing he had seen in a long time, Harsh thought. She stopped when she saw him.

"Say there, don't stop on my account."

"I was just getting a bit of exercise and letting off steam."

"Don't stop. I don't know much about that game, but you must be pretty good. I enjoyed watching you."

"I'm out of practice, I am afraid."

"If that was being rusty, you must be something when you got the shine on."

"Care to try it?" Miss Muirz tossed him a ball. He found it to be near the size of a baseball and hard as a rock. Miss Muirz stood beside him. "The glove on my *cesta* can be let out a little to fit your hand."

"Oh, no, thanks. Not me. You know a ball like this could kill a man if he got beaned with it, which would be just my luck."

"Do not be chicken."

"Is that what you call the thing, a *cesta*?"

"Yes."

"I bet it would be harder to learn to use than a snow-shoe."

"You are chicken, aren't you?"

"Nah. But don't say I didn't warn you." He let her fasten the basket device on his right hand. She smelled faintly of perfume. His shoulder touched hers. She put the ball in the basket and he hauled off and let fly and missed the wall entirely. The ball disappeared. That ball went to hell and gone off into the mangroves, he thought, abashed. He indicated his left arm with a motion of his head. It still hung from its sling. "Bum arm overbalanced me, I guess."

He watched her from the corner of his eye and saw she was not amused. She was not irritated either. She was just indifferent. He didn't like that she was indifferent, he realized. He would like to do a little warming up there.

"You tried to overdo it, Mr. Harsh."

"I guess. There's more to this than a person would think, I can see that now. How did you get so good at it?"

"Once I was a professional."

He looked at the ground, pretending his feelings were damaged. "Say, you set me up for a laugh, didn't you?"

"I just thought you might like to try."

"Yeah, I bet. You know how you made me feel? Like I had tried to show a fellow how to burn one across home plate, and the fellow turned out to be Dizzy Dean or somebody."

She looked at him and he thought he detected a hint of something in her eyes, something that smacked of interest. Remember who you look like, he thought. She knows you're not him, but that doesn't mean she's immune to whatever feelings the sight of him might stir up.

She spoke gently. "I am sorry to make you feel bad."

"Oh, I'll get over it. But seeing as how you made me feel about two inches tall, I think you ought to do something to raise me back to size. Something like riding into town with me and having dinner this evening."

She shook her head quickly. "It is not wise for you to leave the estate."

"Yeah, but you can't leave me two inches high."

She smiled. "No, I can hardly do that, can I?"

"We're on, then?"

She shook her head again. "I don't say I wouldn't like

it, Mr. Harsh. An evening away from here. From them. But no, we cannot leave the estate without a good reason."

"Well, I got a good reason. You see, I got nothing to wear, no clothes for this climate, and certainly none for this part you people want me to play. I got to go into town and buy some stuff."

"We can send someone to buy you clothes."

"Not so as they'd fit properly."

"They'd fit well enough."

"For bumming on the beach maybe. But what about when you want to trot me out as your *El Presidente?* Did he go around in beachwear? Or suits that didn't fit him just right?" He saw her nod slightly in agreement. "Anyway I'm damned if I am going to think of myself as a prisoner here."

"You are not a prisoner, Harsh, but you do look exactly like a man who is being searched for all the world over. Really, it would be best if you stayed out of sight."

"We could cover up my face. I could wear a scarf, a hat. Plus I've still got this bandage on, so you can't see practically half my face. And I'd stay indoors most of the time, I wouldn't be walking around on the street. It'd be quick, too—an hour, two tops."

"I do not know that the others will have confidence that you would be so careful, Mr. Harsh, or so quick. Or, frankly, that you would necessarily come back at all."

"But what if you went along with me? It would be okay with everybody then, wouldn't it?"

She put one hand out, laid it against his chest. "I'll tell you what, Mr. Harsh. You let me talk to the others, and I'll see what they think. Maybe it can be arranged. Maybe.

However, if I do get permission to take you into town, you must promise to stay out of sight as much as possible. We would go straight to a men's clothing store, then straight back, and no dining in public restaurants. If you want dinner with me, we shall have it here."

"Say, now we're getting somewhere."

SEVENTEEN

When Miss Muirz came out of the house for the trip into Palm Beach, she wore a grey dress which made her look tall, a grey hat, plain grey pumps. The only things not grey were her belt and a big handbag, which were shades of brown. They took the limousine. She drove. The machine had a partition between the front seats and the rear section, so they both sat in front.

"Will you open the gate?" Miss Muirz pulled the car to a halt just shy of the metal gate separating the driveway from the main road.

"Glad to, if you give me the key."

Miss Muirz shook her head. "You don't need a key. They don't keep it locked."

Harsh didn't say anything to that, just got out and opened it, then closed it after she'd driven through. He got back in the limousine. He would remember about the gate being unlocked, he thought. It would be important if he had to make a break later.

They followed a road that wound south about a mile through sand and mangroves. The sea was quite near to the left. In many spots sand had drifted across the black-top. Other large estates began to appear near the road just before it swung westward and joined another road coming in from the south. They crossed a causeway, then a drawbridge, and fifteen minutes put them in Palm Beach.

The store where they stopped was expensive looking, a one-story cream-colored building with a simple neon sign saying LEON in script. "This is a very fine men's shop." Miss Muirz pulled up at a side street door. "Brother says so, anyway."

They went inside and a salesman in a mess jacket and cummerbund and black trousers began showing them slacks and the trimmings. When the man first looked at him after Harsh unwound the scarf from the lower part of his face, Harsh was nervous about what his reaction would be. Would there be a look of recognition followed by a hastily made excuse for leaving the room, then the sound of a phone receiver carefully being lifted from its hook? But no—the man showed no sign of recognizing him at all. Not everyone listened to the radio, he supposed. Or maybe the newspapers hadn't had a chance to put photos out yet.

The sales clerk gestured for them to follow him toward the back of the store. Looking at the clothing on the racks they were passing, Harsh could find no price tags. "Jeez, they're afraid to let you see the prices in this joint."

Miss Muirz whispered in his ear. "Don't worry about it. It will go on the expense account. Anything you want."

"Somebody got generous, huh?"

"You made a persuasive argument, Harsh. We need you to look the part."

Well, what the hell, Harsh decided. He had better load up on clothes while the offer stood. Slacks and Bermuda shorts, sport shirts, a couple of tropical-weight suits, a summer tux, all the accessories. Trying the suit jackets on with one arm still in a cast wasn't easy, but with help from

the other two he managed to get them on halfway. He
wound up with a pile of merchandise stacked in front of
him. He made sure to work in some slacks and a sport
coat which needed alterations.

For the alterations he was escorted into the tailoring
room in the rear where the dressing booths were. The
booth assigned him was near a window that gave a view of
the side street where the limousine was parked.

"Hey, buddy, you got a telephone back here?" Harsh
winked and jerked his head toward the front of the store
where Miss Muirz had remained. "A private phone, if
you get what I mean." The clerk returned the conspir-
ator's wink and opened a cabinet on the wall between the
window and a back door held shut with a hook-and-eye
latch. Inside the cabinet there was a phone on a small
shelf and a dog-eared Yellow Pages beside it.

Harsh went to the telephone. Before he picked up the
instrument, he lighted a cigarette. He was very nervous
and did not want it to be noticed. He wished he had been
more subtle about getting to the phone, and had left out
that remark about privacy. The clerk would remember
something like that.

Suddenly Harsh also realized he did not recall the telephone number of the Security Locksmithing Company.
He thought he had memorized the number until it would
never go out of his mind. Damn! He picked up the directory and thumbed through it one-handed till he found
the number, then discovered he was too nervous to trust
himself to remember it long enough to dial it. So he
wrote it on the front of the phone book in pencil. The
window beside the telephone admitted blinding Florida

sunshine, and he had to squint as he wrote. There was too damn much sunshine in Florida.

He dialed the number. Then he watched the people coming and going in the street below while the phone rang. He felt conspicuous in front of the big window. He noticed one tourist, a man with an enormously floppy straw hat and sunglasses, at an orange stand across the street, sipping something through a straw. It was hard to tell because of the sunglasses, but it looked like the man was staring this way. The hell with you, you curious bastard, Harsh thought, turning his back.

In his ear, the ringing stopped as the phone finally was answered. A gruff voice spoke. "Security."

Harsh drew in breath. "Who is this?"

The voice answered wearily. "Goldberg."

Harsh reminded himself to stay calm and not arouse anybody's suspicions. "Mr. Goldberg, do you open safes?"

"Yes, that's our business."

"I mean are you the man who actually does the work on the safes, because what I want is some technical information."

"I'm the only one here, mister. I do my own locksmithing. What did you say your name is?"

Harsh kept his tone casual. "Fry. Edward Fry. Now here's my problem, Mr. Goldberg. I have a wall safe in my house, see. One of them safes with an inner door that opens with a couple of keys at once. The problem is, I lost one key. The combination to the outer door and one key is all I got, which don't get me in my safe. I was wondering, could you folks fix me up?"

"You want to open the safe, is that it?"

"Well, if it doesn't run into a lot of expense. Could you give me an idea what it would cost?" Harsh felt that bringing up cost would keep Goldberg from thinking anything was shady.

"I would need more information about your safe before I could tell you much over the telephone."

Harsh gave Goldberg the name of the safe company, *Monitor Safe Corporation, Boston, Mass.*, and the number he'd found etched near the bottom of the safe door, which was 3A. Harsh then got out the key Brother had given him and read the tiny numbers stamped onto it, 3301-7-2. "Is that any help to you, Mr. Goldberg?"

"Oh, yes. Yes, I think you have a rather simple problem, Mr. Fry. From those numbers we can make you a duplicate key. We won't need anything else."

"I don't need a duplicate of this key I got. It's the one I lost that I want replaced."

"That's what I mean. Notice the last figures in the key number you gave me, the figures seven and two? Well, those are guide figures, and from them, and from information we have in our files, we can duplicate the lost key for you."

"Say, that sounds all right. But what will it cost me?"

"Twenty-five dollars."

"Jesus creeping Christ, for twenty-five bucks I could buy a new safe, damn near."

"You make some inquiries, Mr. Fry, and you will find our figure to be standard. We have our expenses, our bonding, and so on. We have many expenses you would not think a locksmith would have."

"But Jesus Christ, twenty-five dollars."

"Well, at the same time the price is only one dollar

each for additional copies of the key, because we have our set-up made."

"Mr. Goldberg, I was expecting maybe a couple of bucks for a key. But if you say twenty-five is reasonable, maybe we better go ahead and you make me the key. I'll send you the twenty-five and you mail me the key, okay?"

"I am afraid it's not that simple, Mr. Fry. I couldn't mail the key."

"How is that?"

"You will have to personally appear and sign an affidavit. Just a formality, but it's the law."

Here was where Goldberg was going to get suspicious if care was not used, Harsh thought. "Oh, well, sure. I didn't know you had to have an affidavit. I can see reasons for that. I'll be glad to sign your papers. When could I come around and sign it and get the key?"

"Any time after tomorrow noon, Mr. Fry."

"After noon tomorrow, that will be fine, Mr. Goldberg. I don't know exactly when it will be convenient for me to drop around, but you go ahead with the key and I will see you soon."

Miss Muirz smoked her cigarette in a long holder. She had picked out for Harsh a large checkered cap, which she suggested that he try on, and which he felt made him look as if he was wearing the lid from a milk can. But standing beside him in the full-length mirror's reflection Miss Muirz was very lovely and elegant looking. So the hell with what the hat looked like.

"I'm sorry it took them so long to fit me, Miss Muirz. I got a thin waist and they had to take in the stuff. God, do I have to say I like this cap?"

She said he did not have the Continental touch with clothes, then set the cap aside and gave him back the hat he'd worn into the store. He pulled it down over his brow while she went and paid the bill. He wondered what the Continental touch was. The bill came to over five hundred dollars. The salesman personally carried all the stuff out to the car in one medium-sized armload, all but the garments left for alterations. A clip joint, Harsh thought, but rather fancy at that. If he ever got the wall safe open, he might make a habit of such toggeries.

It was getting dark, becoming a beautiful evening. Everything glowed like satin from the twilight and the air was not as warm as it had been. The breeze was lazy and filled with the perfume of tropical blooms and the engine of the limousine ran quietly as if half-asleep. Harsh felt fine. "Where do we eat?"

"We do not go to a restaurant, Mr. Harsh. I told you that, and you promised."

"Hell, I knew you weren't serious. I knew that was just for the others to hear, and we were going to make an evening of it."

She shook her head. "You did not know anything of the kind."

"You are ruining my life, did you know that?"

She drove the big limousine expertly. The car turned south on a boulevard and passed small houses, service stations, drive-ins. The lights of a supermarket made a Christmas-tree-like display ahead.

"Oh my God, let's be reasonable, Miss Muirz. Let's at least stop and get a couple steaks at that place ahead. I can cook a fine steak on the beach, if you're so afraid somebody will see us."

To his astonishment she shrugged and turned in at the supermarket and parked in the rear where there were no other cars. "You must not get out, Mr. Harsh." She went inside the supermarket.

Man oh man, Harsh thought, and he leaned back on the seat and felt of the left side of his face and the arm in its sling. Both felt all right except for some itching, which he supposed was a good sign. Man oh man, he was almost afraid to think how well the afternoon was going. The telephone call to the Security Locksmithing Company had come off perfectly. Miss Muirz was showing signs of cooperation. This could turn into one hell of a day, that was what it could do.

Miss Muirz purchased some steaks, romaine, frozen French fries, and a bottle of brandy. She showed him the steaks.

"Say, they make my mouth water."

"Mine, too."

Now she drove the limousine at greater speed. The wind, cool and hard as glass pressing against their faces, rushed in the open windows. They crossed the causeway and drawbridge over black water with winking buoy lights on its surface. The strong breathing of the engine, the lime whiteness of the headlights, gave Harsh a feeling he was in a detached and fast-moving world. Miss Muirz turned into the stretch of blacktop road which followed the beach back to the estate. Now there were no houses nearby.

Harsh reached over and turned off the ignition. He seized the wheel and steered the limousine to a stop at the edge of the road. There was an interval of silence after the car halted. Either Miss Muirz or the inside of the limousine smelled faintly of jasmine.

"Mr. Harsh, why did you do that?"

"I guess I was just overcome. You know what? You and I are going to park right here and take those steaks down to the beach and broil them on a driftwood fire. We are going to have us a picnic, that is what we are going to do."

"I do not think we should."

"Come on, come on. A fire by the oceanside, broiled steaks, a slug of brandy and thou, as the poet would say."

"Mr. Harsh, we cannot do that."

"Look Miss Muirz, you can see I'm easy to get along with. I wanted to eat out, hit a classy restaurant, but you said no, and I went along with what you wanted. I did that because I can see where you folks might not want me to be seen around too much. But this is different. Do you see any crowds around here? It's a half mile to the nearest house. Who's to see us?"

She leaned back. Her hands were resting on the steering wheel. "You know something, Mr. Harsh?" She cleared her throat. "You scared me badly when you stopped the car the way you did."

"How was that?"

"There has been a car tailing us, and I thought it was closing in on us." She brushed the hair back over her ears. "I thought we were going to have to get out of the car and run away in the darkness to save our lives."

"Is that so?" Harsh did not believe there had been a car tailing them. "Is that so, now?" Harsh turned and looked back. He did not see any signs of another car. "You can think up a better one, Miss Muirz, can't you?"

"I am very serious."

She sounded convincing and Harsh turned around to stare backward a second time. "Don't see anyone." He realized she was reaching to turn the key in the ignition. "I thought so." He put his hand over hers. "Now that was a schoolgirl way to act, Miss Muirz, kidding me along like that. What if you had scared me into having a heart attack?"

"But we *are* being followed."

"Let 'em follow, let 'em come!" Harsh made a theatrical gesture. "Bring on the mystery enemy, I am prepared and without fear."

Miss Muirz jerked her hand from under his. "Listen, you big ape! I would like to broil a steak with you on the beach. I really mean that. But we are being followed."

"Yeah. Yeah, I know." Harsh took hold of her hands in one of his, and the instant he had hold of them, he knew that they would or they wouldn't and either way it was going to be exciting. Her hands were like warm excited cats.

"Watch out, Mr. Harsh."

"That's what I'm gonna do, baby. That's what—"

Godamighty, there *was* a car behind! He lifted his head, looked back. The car, coming without lights, was almost on them. With an outcry from locked wheels, it came to a stop. It was a small convertible two-seater sports car which Harsh had seen at Brother's estate. Mr. Hassam was driving. Brother stood up in the little car and jumped over the side. He had the shotgun in his hands.

Harsh shoved Miss Muirz, hoping to get her out on the driver's side of the car, so he could leave by the same route. This would put him on the limousine opposite side to Brother, give him a chance for his life, he felt. But she didn't move, and when he looked over at her he discovered Miss Muirz was holding a revolver, a big thing, a

Magnum such as he had seen state patrolmen wearing.
Miss Muirz let the gun rest on her knee. It was as ugly as
a black hog. Brother jerked open the car door, the shotgun
in his other hand. Harsh turned on the seat and brought
up his legs and kicked Brother in the face with both feet.
Brother fell like a quarter of beef. Harsh slid out of the
car and he was groping for the shotgun when Mr. Hassam
touched his shoulder. "What in God's name did you do
that for? Why did you kick him?"

"He was gonna shoot us, the son of a bitch." Fright
made Harsh's voice quite hoarse.

"No, he thought you were in trouble." Mr. Hassam
sounded disgusted. "We saw your car stop and the lights
go out, and we thought you were ambushed."

"The hell!" Harsh leaned against the limousine weakly.
"Why didn't you say so?" His legs felt double-jointed. "I
thought Brother was going to shoot us both. He has been
pretty free with that shotgun once before, you know."

Miss Muirz had gotten out of the limousine. She carried the big revolver lightly. "Hassam, was that you trailing
us from town?"

"No. Not from town. We were parked at the road junc-
tion and we saw you pass, then we saw another car pass
behind you. We decided it could be following you, so we
fell in behind."

"Where did the other car go?"

"It turned off on the beach, apparently."

"We had better look into the matter of that car." Miss
Muirz sounded calm and deadly.

"I never saw anybody following us from town." Harsh
wiped his forehead.

Miss Muirz gave him a look. "You had something else on your mind."

She walked back along the road and Mr. Hassam picked up Brother's shotgun and followed her. Harsh fell in behind. The quick succession of events had shaken him, the way Miss Muirz had produced the big revolver shaking him as much as anything.

They walked some three hundred yards and found a parked car. It was a small sedan, and Mr. Hassam circled it cautiously, his feet noiseless in the sand. "No one here." He put a hand on the radiator. "Warm." The shotgun made an audible noise as he cocked it. "Shall we have a look at the beach?"

On the beach they saw several persons, a man and a woman who were sitting by a driftwood fire toasting something, other men fishing in the surf with casting rods.

They watched these people from cover for some time. Mr. Hassam made a disgusted sound. "We are not going to be sure of anything."

"Maybe it was just some guy goin' fishin'." Harsh found his mouth was dry.

Miss Muirz put the big revolver away in her purse. So that was where it had come from, Harsh thought. Mr. Hassam dropped the shotgun in the crook of his arm after uncocking it. "If that bastard was not on the gunboat in the harbor at home, I know who I would suspect it was. But—well, it may have been a fisherman." He turned and trudged off through the sand toward the limousine and the sports car. Miss Muirz and Harsh followed. The walk was silently thoughtful.

Brother had recovered consciousness. He had climbed into the back of the limousine and was leaning back holding a handkerchief to his mouth. He got out of the car shakily when he heard them coming, and seemed prepared for flight. He recognized them. He gave Harsh a wry look. "You pack a lusty kick, Mr. Harsh."

Harsh was astonished by the man's politeness. "I guess I picked the wrong time to let go with it." Harsh felt almost apologetic.

EIGHTEEN

The sunrises and sunsets around here were some shows, Harsh thought as he stood looking out of his bedroom window the next morning at the purple clouds stacked in front of the sun, great mountains of them with the sun behind like a golden furnace reflecting rich yellow around the edges of the clouds and into the canyons between. The sea was serge blue and each wave bore a sparkling crest as it came in from the horizon. The waves dumped fifty-foot-wide sheets of foam on the sand around the feet of the tiny long-legged birds that ran up and down the beach.

He did some experimental exercises with his left arm and decided it did not feel bad. He could flex the fingers without pain. His eyelids were gummy and he picked at one of them with a fingernail and pulled cautiously at the sleep stuff that was stuck to the eyelashes.

He reviewed last night. He decided that no person or persons unknown had been trailing himself and Miss Muirz. That was baloney. Mr. Hassam and Brother had got their wind up, was all. There had probably been some guy and his gal in the car they had found with the warm radiator, but almost any time of the day or night you could hear people whooping it up on the beaches near the estate.

He wished Mr. Hassam and Brother had not shown up last night, because they had sure queered his plans for

Miss Muirz. Why couldn't the silly bastards stay away when they weren't wanted, he thought.

He went to the wall near the safe and put a cheek against the plaster and looked behind the oil painting for the match head. It was still in place, so no one had tampered with the safe. He felt like laughing as he wondered if Goldberg was working on that key yet.

Then he thought of something that made him feel sick. Jesus, he was dumb! There last night he had walked off and left Brother alone unconscious, and Brother probably had the other safe key on his person at the time. Jesus, why hadn't he thought of that, how stupid could he get? What a dumb thing, to go following Miss Muirz and Mr. Hassam off down the beach, taking a chance of getting his head shot off, when he might have stayed behind and filched the key off Brother while he was senseless.

He was disgusted with himself. He went to the portable bar and poured bourbon into a glass and drank it, and the liquor promptly tied his empty stomach in a knot and brought tears to his eyes. A guy as dumb as he had been last night deserved to choke to death, he thought bitterly.

When Harsh had dressed, he went down to breakfast, and found Vera Sue sitting on the dining terrace. When he saw her, it was too late to retreat.

Vera Sue planted her knife and fork on the table with a bang. "Walter, I think you are the biggest stinker that ever lived."

He was somewhat relieved, having expected her to scream and throw something. "I guess you're right, Vera Sue."

"You know what I'm mad about, Walter?"

"Yeah, I guess I know."

"You robbed me. While I was asleep, you took my money, didn't you?"

"Well, I guess I must have. Anyway I found some dough in my pocket the next morning, and I didn't remember where it came from."

"Walter, I bet you split open your head trying to remember where you got the money. I just bet you did."

She lit her cigarette with elaborate gestures which led him to suspect she had already taken a drink or two.

"Gosh, baby, I knew where it must have come from. But what could I do? I knew it was the liquor made me do it, you know how it is with me, I get to drinking. I pull some awfully hot ones. It was the damn Benedictine, I guess, I don't know. Anyway, I still got it all and you can have it back if you want, but I wish you would let me have ten bucks temporarily, so I wouldn't be flat. Or maybe twenty-five."

"Damn you, you want to keep it all anyway, don't you?"

The servant who was serving breakfast asked Harsh what he would have. Harsh told him anything would do.

When the servant left, Vera Sue sighed. "Walter, this is one peach of a place, but it gets me down. The servants, a regular goddamn mansion and all, I should have myself the time of my life. But nobody gives a hoot about me. They hardly speak to me, anybody, including you."

"Vera Sue, I been afraid to say anything to you. I was afraid you would do exactly what you should do, pick up the first thing handy and whock me good."

"Is that the only reason you ignored me?"

"Well, ain't it enough? I been working like a dog anyway, of course. You may have noticed me and Mr. Hassam on the beach a lot. We really been going at it."

Vera Sue jabbed her cigarette into her cup of coffee. "I noticed you went off with that Miss Muirz yesterday and didn't get back until after dark."

"Yes, we made a little business trip."

"You mean a monkey business trip, don't you?"

"No, absolutely not, Vera Sue. Straight business. Mr. Hassam and Brother and Doc Englaster and I been working like mad getting plans for the factory that is going to make my photographic film emulsion. Well, right now we got to a point where we need to send some telegrams to outfits who might be interested in building the factory, and I went into town to send the telegrams. Miss Muirz just drove the car."

Vera Sue frowned. "How come I hear nothing about this photographic factory?"

"Why, it's a big secret. I told you it was a big secret, didn't I? Listen, you mustn't say a word to anybody about it, because they'd have a green hemorrhage if they knew I told you or anyone else."

The servant brought Harsh's coffee. He arranged a plate and silverware. Vera Sue was eyeing the bandage on Harsh's face thoughtfully. The servant departed.

"Walter, what happened to your face?"

"Huh? Oh, that, my face. Well you see I fell and cut my face, but it don't amount to anything much."

"I was thinking about that photograph I saw of the fellow who looked a lot like you, Walter, only he had a scar on his face about where that bandage is on yours."

He laughed loudly at her. "Jesus, you get some tall ideas, don't you?"

°

When Mr. Hassam joined them on the dining terrace, he gave Vera Sue a courtly bow and complimented her on how nice she looked. Vera Sue listened, but her rosebud mouth was pouting, and she decided to get even with Harsh. "Walter was just telling me that the photographic emulsion project is coming along fine."

Harsh promptly kicked her shin under the table, causing her to jump. Mr. Hassam understood perfectly. He looked to Vera Sue seriously. "Well now, Miss Crosby, I would prefer no one discussed that." He sat down and began to talk about the weather and that was the subject for the rest of breakfast.

"Thanks, pal." Harsh was walking with Mr. Hassam to the beach cabana to resume Spanish instruction.

"What was she talking about, Mr. Harsh?"

Harsh told about the lie he had fed Vera Sue about the invention of a photographic emulsion. "What she doesn't know won't hurt anybody. It was nice of you to pick up the cue. You are the one guy around here I feel I can halfway understand, Mr. Hassam. I respect you a lot."

"I appreciate that, Harsh." They reached the beach. Mr. Hassam seemed in no hurry to start on the Spanish. He picked up a stick and threw it out into the surf.

"Are you worried about something, Mr. Hassam?"

"Well, just the thing last night."

"There was nothing to that."

"Maybe. We can hope so, anyway."

"Mr. Hassam, the next time you guys get a wild hair up your ass I wish you would do it when I am not making a play for Miss Muirz. You sure popped off some plans I had last night."

Mr. Hassam grinned faintly. "I did not know we preserved your manhood as well." He began to poke with another stick at objects which resembled small purplish balloons with roots hanging to them. These were floating in from the sea and the waterline was speckled with them. Mr. Hassam lifted one on the stick and suggested Harsh touch it, which he did, and his fingers tingled as if he had dipped them in a mild acid. Mr. Hassam threw the thing back in the water. "Portuguese Man O'War. Spectacular to look at, but another thing to fondle." He looked thoughtfully at Harsh. "But you are the kind of man who likes to find out those things for himself. I do not suppose Miss Muirz will object to the explorations."

"Thanks."

"But there must be no more trips to town. Too risky."

"Yeah? I don't think so." Harsh shook his head. "You are a nice guy and I don't want to argue with you, Mr. Hassam, but I am not a prisoner here. I'm not in any chain gang. I tell you one thing for sure, I am going back to town this afternoon and get the rest of my new clothes, which I left at the place to be altered."

"No."

"Look, goddamn it, Mr. Hassam, what's eating you? Are you afraid I'll throw in with Miss Muirz instead of you? Is that why you don't want me out of sight with her? Well, you're wrong, old buddy, you're wrong, and to prove it, I would rather have you ride into town with me this afternoon than her. How is that?"

Mr. Hassam thought this over. "What time will your garments be ready?"

"About three o'clock."

"I will ride in with you then." Mr. Hassam smiled. "I am taking you up on your bluff, you see."

By three o'clock Harsh had worked out a plan, and although it would take some luck to make the plan click, it was the best thing he could think up, and he felt he would have to chance getting the break. He had most of the details clear in his mind, working them out during the rest periods in the Spanish instruction. The essence of the plan was that he would pick up the wall safe key from Goldberg without Mr. Hassam knowing.

When they arrived at Leon's, Harsh indicated the side street where Miss Muirz had left the limousine yesterday, and Mr. Hassam agreed it was a good secluded spot for parking. Harsh wanted to smile. So far, okay. The limousine was out of sight of the salesroom when it was parked there, but in plain view from the fitting room window.

The next step, keeping Mr. Hassam from entering the fitting room with him, he arranged nicely by pointing out some fabrics to Mr. Hassam and saying how wonderful the fat man would look in a suit made of the cloth. That was enough for the salesman; he tied into Mr. Hassam, unrolling bolts of cloth for his inspection.

"I'll try my stuff on, Mr. Hassam, while you're looking over samples."

"Yes. Very well."

That got him back in the fitting room without Mr. Hassam, and he went to the telephone at once. With the phone number penciled on the directory cover, he didn't even have to take a minute to look it up before dialing the Security Locksmithing Company.

"Hello, Security? Is Goldberg around?"

There was a pause. "Speaking."

"Edward Fry here, Goldberg. I called yesterday about needing a key. You remember?"

"Oh, yes…Fry. We have your key here waiting for you." The man's voice wasn't gruff this time, Harsh noted. No, when he had twenty-five dollars to collect he was all solicitous and honey-voiced, almost sounded like a different person entirely.

"Well that's why I'm calling, Goldberg. The way it is, I've been tied up all day, and it doesn't look as though I can get away for quite a while yet. I was wondering, could you deliver the key right away to me here in town, so I wouldn't have to let go of this hot business prospect I'm working on? I'm trying to put the screw in the guy."

"I guess I could do that, Mr. Fry, depending on where you are."

"Do you know Leon's, the men's place?"

"Certainly. That's only about four blocks from here."

"Oh, that close. That's fine. In the side street on the north side of Leon's place you will find a large limousine parked. It's my car, and I can see it from the window of this place where I'm tied up in conference. Suppose you come over in the next few minutes and bring the key. When you get here, sort of lean on the limousine and I'll be watching and I'll come down, get the key and pay you. Oh yes, and sign your paper. Bring your paper along. That way I won't lose but a minute or two. Can you accommodate me that much, Goldberg?"

"Of course. I will be right over, Mr. Fry."

Harsh hung up, went to the nearest fitting booth, put on one of the pairs of pants he'd left to be altered, and seizing the fabric of the slacks at the crotch, pulled a bag into the cloth. Then he walked out to show Mr. Hassam they were too full and put up a holler, demanding the slacks be fixed right now while they waited. That was to get him more time, time enough to get the key from Goldberg, and also make sure Mr. Hassam was not going to pop up looking to leave while he was down in the street getting the key.

Back in the fitting rooms, Harsh glued himself to the window. He unlatched the hook-and-eye keeping the back door shut and kept his hand on the doorknob.

Presently a solid-looking man about Harsh's build wearing a gabardine suit and sport shirt came from the north and stopped walking when he saw the limousine. The man wore dark sunglasses and had on a large straw hat, and Harsh recognized him from the day before: the tourist, the one who'd been watching from the orange stand across the way. Goddamn it, of all the times for him to show up—

The man stopped beside the limousine, looked it over, then walked around to the back and glanced at the license plate. He wrote the license number in a notebook. Then he opened the back door and got into the limousine.

Harsh hurried out the side door and strode to the limousine. Some sort of cop, for sure. The regular sort or maybe a private cop, like the guy from Kansas City. Writing the license number down, the nosy bastard.

Harsh flung the car door open. "What the hell, get out of there, you. This is my car."

The man was sitting on the long padded bench in the back of the limousine. Though it was dark inside he hadn't taken off the sunglasses or the hat. He held up a key strung on a piece of twine. "That what you wanted?"

The honeyed voice was familiar to Harsh from the phone and the key looked like the one Brother had given him, the one he was now carrying alongside the money in his pocket. But this guy couldn't be Goldberg. It was impossible. He'd spoken to Goldberg on the phone yesterday while this guy was at the orange stand, watching through the window.

But—

But he could have found out I called Goldberg, Harsh realized. It wouldn't have been hard, if the cop was any good at his job. All he'd have needed to do was come into Leon's sometime after Harsh had left, go back to the fitting rooms, take a look at the phone book, and there was Goldberg's number penciled right on the cover. Hell, he might have seen me writing it, Harsh thought bitterly. And if he called the number and went over to Goldberg's shop, forced Goldberg to tell him what the call had been about, waited there for Harsh to call again…

Harsh reached out and took the key. His hand shook.

The cop had a sour breath and he seemed to be panting gently. Something wrong with him, Harsh decided, maybe a little sick or something.

Harsh wondered how far the man would take the masquerade. "Okay…Goldberg. Give me your paper and I'll give you the money." Harsh held out twenty-five dollars of Vera Sue's money which he had counted out and had ready. The man took it and handed back a printed form. Must've picked it up from Goldberg, Harsh figured, the same time as he picked up the key. Harsh scribbled *Edward T. Fry* at the bottom, on a line where there was a penciled X. "Well, Goldberg, I guess that does it. I'll let you know if the key don't do the job."

The man spoke woodenly. "One more thing. May I see your driver's license?"

"Huh?"

"Your driver's license, please. Let me see some identification, Fry."

I *bet* you'd like to see my identification, you bastard. "Look...Goldberg...I can afford a chauffeur to drive this car, so what the hell would I be doing carrying a driver's license that I don't need? I haven't packed a driver's license around with me in years."

"But I need to confirm your identity. Some cards will do. Some business cards, no? Just show me something that says on it the name of Edward T. Fry."

"Listen, my wallet is upstairs in the office and I am damn well not going to run up there and get it just because you want to see something that doesn't amount to a damn anyway. The hell with you, mister, you and I are done with our business."

Harsh started to get out of the car. The man seized him by the shoulders with both hands. The fellow was surprisingly strong. Harsh's left arm twinged with pain beneath his grip. "We are not done. You will tell me who you are. That face of yours—"

"I'll tell you just once, friend, take your goddamn hands off me. I don't care who you are, cop or P.I. or what."

"You will tell me, all right, but it will be what I want to know. Who are you and what are you plotting to do?"

The use of the word *plotting* put a coldness into Harsh's midriff. "I told you to take your hands off me." Harsh gave the man the edge of his hand the way they had taught him in the army, the edge of the hand delivered hard from a bent elbow against the man's throat just below the Adam's apple. The man fell down on the floor between the front and back seats. He lay at Harsh's feet, not knocked out, but paralyzed with pain, unable to speak, barely able to breathe.

Now what happens? Harsh thought. Will a good kick or two in the gut send him away happy to leave me alone? Harsh looked down at the man squirming on the floor. Suddenly he saw the man tugging at a coat pocket. Oh Jesus, Harsh thought, a gun, a gun in his pocket. Harsh pulled back one foot and stamped on the man's face, causing something to crush, a jawbone or something. He stomped again on the man's belly, and this threw air out of the man's lungs and a spray of blood and spittle across the floor carpeting of the limousine. He's not so tough, Harsh thought. They used to make cops of harder stuff. It was not going to be difficult to render the man senseless, then drag him into an alley and leave him until Harsh could re-join Mr. Hassam and clear out of the vicinity. It would serve the fellow right to wind up in an alley. What else could he expect for being a nosy bastard?

Harsh realized he was feeling about the man the way he always commenced feeling about someone with whom he was in trouble. The first occasion he'd had such a feeling, and he remembered it very well, was as a kid in a fight with another kid, one of the earliest things he could recall, a fight with a kid eight years old, about his age, back of the outhouse in the country schoolyard near Novelty, Missouri. A fight with a kid who was a teacher's pet, who had come upon Harsh getting an eyeful at a

crack in the girls' donnicker and yelled he would tell
their teacher on him. Harsh could not remember who
won the fight, which was rather odd; the only thing he
could recall, and he recalled it vividly, was the feeling
that came over him of nothing mattering except reducing
the opponent to helplessness. It was not winning that was
important, it was reducing the opposition to complete
nothingness.

This was the feeling he had now. He was stamping the
man with both feet simultaneously. The man's right hand
was still in his coat pocket groping about there, and Harsh
became sure there was a gun in the pocket when he heard
a metallic object strike the footrail. Christ! Harsh fell
upon the man and seized the coat-pocketed hand with all
his strength. He could feel the gun in the pocket. The
cop was trying to shoot him with it. Harsh twisted the
gun hand, bending it upward and trying to get the arm
twisted against the small of the man's back. If he could
hammerlock the guy, Harsh felt, he could get the gun,
and Jesus Christ he had to get the gun. Harsh strained
every muscle he had, using his cast for leverage. The gun
went off. The noise was a lot, yet not so much either for
a gun, muffled because the gun was wadded in the coat
cloth and Harsh lying on top of it. A big cough, a jolt
against his chest, that was about all. But the cop's legs
shot out stiffly, his whole body gave a heave, then went
limp.

The thing Harsh noticed now was a brassy taste in his
mouth that came from straining with everything he had.
Then there was the smell of the other man's sour breath,
the smell of powder, the sweetish digested smell of stuff
that started coming out of the cop's smashed and bloody

mouth. There was a kind of ringing in Harsh's ears too, and he had to listen through the ringing in order to hear anything. He listened and waited. He waited for someone to come and hoped no one would come, for he knew that what he was lying on was a dead man. And no one came.

He reached into the man's pocket and took out the gun—a small gun, strangely flat, maybe a .22, it was hard to tell in the darkness. He jammed it in his own jacket pocket. He'd get rid of it later. The bigger problem—the thing that would be much harder to get rid of—lay at his feet.

There was a laprobe folded over a rail on the inside of the door, and he spread this over the cop, relieved that there was enough robe to cover the body.

Mr. Hassam was mildly irked with Harsh. "It took you long enough."

Harsh turned around slowly before Mr. Hassam, showing off the pants he'd raced to put on the instant he'd gotten back into the store. "They got them altered, finally. How do you like them? I didn't want to make any more trips to this place. Fit pretty good, huh?"

Mr. Hassam shrugged, for he had grown tired of the efforts of the salesman to sell him something, and the salesman looked discouraged also, so Harsh knew Mr. Hassam had bought nothing. But the salesman was very polite still, as they would always be in such a classy place; he helped them get together the boxes containing Harsh's clothes, and he offered to carry them to the limousine. "Where is your car, gentlemen?"

"Never mind, I can carry the stuff."

"But your arm, sir—"

"I said never mind." Harsh did not want the salesman opening the limousine to put the package in and finding the body in the back seat. "I want to carry them myself."

"Very well. I hope you find everything satisfactory. If not, we will certainly make it right."

"Thanks, buddy."

There were not too many packages this time for Harsh to manage with one arm. The salesman opened the shop door for them. Harsh and Mr. Hassam approached the limousine, and Harsh made his move to keep Mr. Hassam from opening the rear door or even looking in the back.

"Hey, how about me driving this pot back, Mr. Hassam? I bet it will do a hundred and twenty. How about you giving me a chance to try her out on that beach stretch?"

Mr. Hassam hurriedly got behind the wheel. Harsh sighed in relief. He had noted Mr. Hassam was a very cautious driver. Harsh piled boxes on the back seat. Under the laprobe the cop did not make much of a pile. Harsh slammed the back door, got in front with Mr. Hassam. "Okay. Home, James."

The limousine was hardly moving before Harsh noticed the smell in the car, coming from the back. He hurriedly rolled down his window. Mr. Hassam glanced at him. "You feeling all right, Harsh?"

"Huh? Me, oh sure, I guess twisting around with this busted arm to try on them clothes got me sweating a little is all. Sure, I'm fine."

At the supermarket where Miss Muirz had turned in last night, Mr. Hassam also stopped. "I have to pick up some groceries, Harsh."

"Okay. Suppose I stay here in the car. No point in

being seen around any more than necessary, is there?"

Mr. Hassam parked in the back about where Miss Muirz had parked the previous night. "This should take only fifteen minutes or so, Harsh." Mr. Hassam entered the market. Harsh sat very still, thinking over what had happened. He was not sweating or shaking or anything. He wondered if anyone had noticed anything. He hoped not. Who notices a parked car on a city street, he thought, and the answer he gave himself was, nobody, mostly. The gun had not made much of a disturbance, and neither had the cop. Harsh felt pretty good about it as a whole. But he reminded himself he could be sliding over a detail and not know it. He kept thinking.

The printed form that said Edward T. Fry was the legal owner of the safe for which the key had been made, that was still in the cop's pocket! Or was it? He had sure better find out—Edward T. Fry might be a made-up name, but it was signed in Harsh's handwriting. He glanced about to make sure no one was in sight, then opened the sliding panel between the front of the car and the rear seat and leaned through to lift the blanket and put his hand in the cop's pockets. He found the paper. He covered the cop again with the laprobe, drew back into the front seat, struck a match to the paper and waved it about to make it burn rapidly, then fanned the smoke out of the limousine interior.

Now what else? He was very alarmed. He felt he should not have overlooked the printed form, since it had not just his handwriting on it but his fingerprints, too. His fingerprints—Christ, his fingerprints might be on the twenty-five dollars! Did paper even *take* fingerprints? It did if you inked the fingers, that was for sure; and who was to say that sweat didn't show up just the same as ink under some special light bulb the police had? He leaned back through the panel opening again and searched the cop's pockets once more. He found the twenty-five dollars, which he folded and put in his pocket.

And as long as he was at it, he thought, why overlook any spare change the cop might have been packing? He found a large, new-looking folded wallet in the cop's inside coat pocket and took it. He did not dare take time to look at the contents.

Now, anything more? When Mr. Hassam came back with the groceries, where would he put them? In the back seat? If he did, the moment he opened the door he would see the cop's body. The thing to do was to get rid of the body, and fast—he might only have a few minutes left. Harsh glanced about the vicinity again and noticed a tall trash can sitting some twenty feet from the limousine. The can looked promising. It was a large one. Harsh slid over into the driver's seat, started the limousine engine and backed the machine out, sliding it into a new parking spot alongside the trash can.

It should be no trick to put the cop in the trash can, he thought, and he looked once more for anyone who might see him. Two women drove into the lot, parked and went inside the market. Coast clear now, he decided, and he pulled open the back door of the limousine, seized the cop by the legs and dragged the body out until he could get a one-armed grip on it. He only needed to turn around and there was the can. He shoved the lid off the big can with his knee.

The can was full. Level to the top with trash, sweepings, mashed-down cardboard boxes from the supermarket.

Harsh shoved the cop's body back into the limousine, cursing. It was one of the swiftest acts of his life. He wondered if his hair had turned white.

Harsh had the lid to the limousine's trunk open and raised and was standing by it when Mr. Hassam came out of the supermarket carrying two large paper bags. "Hey, put the groceries in here. I don't want my new clothes messed up with the bananas. And how about me driving? I got behind the wheel while you were gone and I moved her back and forth a time or two. She is some boat." Mr. Hassam shook his head and took the driver's wheel rather hastily. "I have not seen a sample of your driving, but I doubt if it is my style."

Harsh got into the limousine. He sat there thinking about how he had stood for a moment with a dead cop hugged to his chest and looked at the packed-full trash can. He shuddered violently, and Mr. Hassam glanced at him. "You couldn't be cold, Harsh? It's nearly ninety degrees."

Harsh shook his head. "It's your damn slowpoke driving. This rod can do a hundred and twenty and still be half-asleep. Why don't you let me slide in behind the wheel, and I'll show you how to let her out."

Mr. Hassam was doing about forty. He cut it down ten.

NINETEEN

When they reached the estate, Harsh had another hard time of it. But by leaping out of the limousine the moment it stopped and getting his own boxes out of the back seat while Mr. Hassam got the sacks of groceries from the trunk, it went all right. At least the body was not found. This can't last, Harsh thought, and he decided to get his money out of the wall safe at once and take off. He wanted out of here, and fast. Although his luck had been clicking, the trouble with a run of luck was that nobody can tell how long it will hang on, or how soon it will turn the other way with the bottom falling out of everything.

As soon as he was in his room, he locked the door, then ran to the wall safe. His first attempt at the combination was a miss. It must be because he was nervous, he reflected; he had opened the outer door with the combination numerous times before. He wiped the sweat off his hands and tried again, successfully this time. All right, now the keys to the inner door. The key Brother had given him and the key that Goldberg had made and the cop had so helpfully delivered. He had put Goldberg's key in his pocket, alongside Brother's. He reached in his pocket for them. His mouth suddenly tasted of brass.

He went though all his pants pockets, slapping, grabbing, finally turning the pockets inside out. Not a thing. Nothing in the way of a key in any pocket. No key. Nothing. Only a knocking that commenced on the door.

❖

Harsh faced the sound of knuckles on the door. "Who's there? What you want?"

"Hassam. Open up, Harsh."

I got to let him in, Harsh thought, I got to act like nothing was wrong with anything anywhere. He closed the outer door of the safe and spun the combination, then he walked over and unfastened the door of his room. "I was getting ready to take a bath."

Mr. Hassam entered bearing a tray holding two glasses and a martini shaker. "You looked as if you needed a drink, so I brought you one."

"Jesus, yes, I can stand one."

"I thought you might." Mr. Hassam poured from the shaker into the glasses. His hand was plump and steady and he filled each glass until the liquid stood fractionally above the edge of the glass. "I saw you were jumpy. A little snort, I said to myself, is what friend Harsh needs. As a matter of fact, I wanted to thank you for being very cooperative on our trip into town."

Harsh looked at the over-full glass. He hesitated to reach for it, feeling he was too nervous to keep from spilling it. However, when he finally picked up the glass and drank from it, he did not lose a drop. He was encouraged. "Say, that hits the spot, Mr. Hassam."

"Too dry for you?"

"No. I always say just waving the vermouth cork over the gin makes it right for a Missouri gentleman." Harsh sat down in an armchair and placed the half-emptied glass on the chair arm. He looked at his outstretched legs and got the odd impression they were encased in a strange pair of slacks of a pattern and color quite unfamiliar.

Now, a little bit at a time, Harsh's stomach became

cold. It was as if he was slowly swallowing ice water. It was coming to him that the slacks he now wore were the ones he'd had re-altered, not the ones he'd worn when he'd gone out to meet the cop. Now he knew where the keys were. When he had gone back into the store after killing the cop, he had taken off his trousers and put on the altered pair to show Mr. Hassam. That was it. The keys were in the slacks he had taken off. And those slacks should be in one of the boxes he had carried home from Leon's.

He wanted to turn his head, look at the boxes. They were lying on the bed. It was an effort to look casually at the martini glass instead. He knew he could not stay in the same room with the suit boxes for long without betraying himself. He stood up, rubbing his stomach.

"Say, Mr. Hassam, when do you suppose they are going to feed us around here?"

Mr. Hassam put his head back to toss the last drops of martini down his throat. "That's the other thing I came to tell you." His eyes held regretfully on the empty martini glass upside down over his mouth. "Tonight Miss Muirz thought a cookout on the beach would be nice." He lowered the glass. "I gather she feels you were disappointed over not getting to cook a steak on the beach last night. The others are already out there. She asked that we join them now."

"Now?" Harsh couldn't help it—he looked at the boxes.

"Yes, now, Harsh. Haven't you spent enough time today trying on clothes? I thought you said you were hungry."

Harsh had to force himself to follow Mr. Hassam to the door.

°

Miss Muirz was building up a fire on the sand, and Doctor Englaster and Brother were scouting firewood. Harsh nudged Mr. Hassam as they approached, figuring it would be best to keep up the appearance that nothing had changed. "Any chance, do you think, of getting some time alone with Miss Muirz? How do I get rid of all the damn chaperones?"

"I'm sure you'll think of something, Harsh. And be my guest, just so you wait until after a talk we are going to have sometime this evening." Mr. Hassam's voice was firm.

"A talk?"

Mr. Hassam nodded. "It's time cards went on the table."

"Hello, there." Miss Muirz picked up a stick of driftwood. "This is the kind of firewood I want, firm and dry, short pieces." She threw that stick down and showed Harsh another stick. "This kind will give off a stink that will make the steaks taste."

She wore tan duck slacks and yellow Chinese sandals with the straps coming out between crimson toenails, and a yellow sheer blouse which reminded Harsh of a puff of sulphur smoke. Her eyebrows had a high thin arch that made them inquisitive, but not amused. Her hair was drawn tight her to her head so that it did not look like hair but like a different-colored skin, and it was fastened in the back with a jeweled comb large enough to be a peacock tail, emeralds and gold like the large earrings pendant from her ears. Her necklace was also emeralds, very large ones which Harsh did not believe were genuine, although he was wrong. She stood close to Harsh. "I thought you would want a steak cooked on the beach. You were so disappointed last night."

The tips of Harsh's ears, the ends of his fingers, felt warm. "I'll help gather the firewood."

They searched in the sand for fuel for the fire and Miss Muirz added it to a blaze under the wire grill. One of the servants brought down two baskets containing the steaks and pickles and silverware and bottles of brandy and glasses, and another brought a beach refrigerator containing cocktail shakers full of drinks already mixed. Both servants retired at once to the house.

Miss Muirz prepared the steak a way Harsh had not seen before. She cut it in thick strips and threaded these on iron rods in S curves with various other items—onion, apple, pineapple, assorted other fruits—then put on soy sauce and herbs. Mr. Hassam made the coffee and some of his ingredients were chocolate, butter, lemon rind, orange rind, cinnamon, bay leaves, Jamaican rum, and brandy. He told Harsh it was an old Arabian desert formula which he had learned before he was five years old. Doctor Englaster stood with his hands on his hips, helping little. Brother sat on the beach listening to a portable radio which he kept on his lap, tuning the radio continuously for news broadcasts.

The wind came off the sea with no more strength than baby breath. The waves arrived in vigorous succession, climbing up and up until there was a wall of water nearly as high as a man rushing up the sand, then falling apart and shooting a sheet of water across the sand under a frosting of bubbles. The bubbles slid about on the wet beach like ice skaters, then were left high and dry, and broke almost audibly.

"Psst!" Brother pointed at the radio he was nursing. "Listen! The news!" He turned up the volume. A commentator's voice came out strongly with deep-throated, resonant tones.

"—demands for his return made by the junta which now controls the government, but these demands are being ignored by the Uruguayans. Unless they accede, El Presidente is safe on the gunboat. But in spite of his advantageous position, the deposed dictator has maintained complete silence. He has made no statement, seen no one, has not appeared publicly. No one we have spoken to in the Uruguayan government will even admit to having seen him, including officials who have made visits to the warship. The only report we have received, and we stress that it is as yet unconfirmed, indicates that the dictator may have sent a courier with a note to a young girlfriend. But there is no concrete proof that El Presidente is on the gunboat. All we know for sure is that the man is in hiding—somewhere. Meanwhile, in the streets of the capitol, a mob today burned thousands of photographs of the former leader and his deceased wife. The tremendous bonfire took place on the Avenida de Libertador General San Martin, the wind carrying the smoke to the harbor even while the shirtless ones trampled the ashes with bare feet. But El Presidente has the last laugh, one commentator noted, since the protestors do not even have shoes while the deposed despot is reputed to have looted millions of dollars worth of government funds and hidden the money abroad.

"Now from London, news of a royal romance…"

Brother shut off the radio.

Miss Muirz looked at Brother irritably. "Why not turn up the volume when the broadcast began? I have friends back home. I would like to know how things are going."

Brother seemed not to hear her. There was a line of moisture across his upper lip and a tremor in his hands as he put the radio on the sand in front of him. "Is he on the gunboat? Is he? Do we know that?"

Mr. Hassam poured straight gin into a glass and handed it to Brother. "In every news report, they bring out that he is supposed to be on the gunboat, yet has not been seen there. I do not like it either."

Brother's teeth made a grinding on the edge of the glass as he drank the gin. He pushed the glass away and lay back on the sand. "I wish he would show up here. I have waited five years for it."

One of Brother's hands came up and wandered around on his chest until it found a shirt button. He unfastened the button, brought out a flat automatic pistol. Brother laid the gun down on his chest over his heart. He put his hand over it. His hand covered the gun completely.

"I will use this." His voice was low and almost sweet. "Is it all right with everyone if I do?"

Doctor Englaster leaned forward. "Is that gun registered here in the States?" Curiosity arched his eyebrows.

"No. No, it is not." Brother was suddenly watching Harsh. "Mr. Harsh—there something wrong with your eyes, Mr. Harsh?"

"Huh?" Harsh took his eyes off the hand Brother had placed over the gun. He'd been thinking it was about the same size as the one the cop had carried—the one still burning a hole in Harsh's jacket pocket. Even looked like a similar make. Apparently his run of luck hadn't ended just yet. "What was that? Nah, there ain't nothing wrong with my eyes."

Brother's hand lifted a few inches, poised motionless above the gun on his chest, then fell back like a tan bird settling on its egg. "Your ears then, perhaps? You heard something that upset you?"

Harsh shrugged. "You trying to pick a fight with me, pal? If it is all right with you, could we wait until after I eat? I fight better on a full stomach."

"What did you stare at, Harsh?"

"That's a pretty nice little gun. Is there a law against looking at it?"

"No. No law."

"Okay."

"Do you want to know where I got this gun, Harsh? It was once his gun—part of his collection. I have had it five years. When I took it, I told him why. I told him I was taking the gun to use later to kill him, and he thought it amusing. Do you suppose the bastard will be amused when I do exactly what I said I would do, shoot him with the gun I took for the purpose five years ago?"

Harsh shrugged. He had seen all he wanted to see of the gun. He leaned back. "Why don't you knock it off, huh?"

Brother's eyes fixed upward, staring ecstatically at the stars. "I hope blood comes out of him, I do want to see his blood. But with these small bullets, I do not know if there will be blood."

"You've certainly got a problem there." Doctor Englaster drank a glass of brandy in its entirety. "A good problem to discuss with our meal. Very appetizing."

Miss Muirz took one of the rods off the grill, waved it around to cool the meat on it, then handed it to Harsh. Harsh took it, but he was not hungry. He pulled some meat off the rod and ate it, then ate the onion and pineapple.

Miss Muirz watched him. She seemed to have the best composure of any of them. It had a glassy quality. "How does it taste, Mr. Harsh?"

Harsh swallowed the meat in his mouth. "Okay. It does taste a little of the conversation, though."

Brother put back his head and laughed weirdly. "Good. Very good, Mr. Harsh. Just like a dead body, eh? You have caught the spirit of our little group, Mr. Harsh."

Doctor Englaster jammed the brandy bottle down in the sand beside him. "Stop it! That's enough of that talk."

Brother stood up and poured coffee in a cup. He tasted it. He poured the coffee out on the sand, and gave them a look of contempt. "Oh, you very normal people. I am going swimming."

"Right after you eat?" Miss Muirz stared at him. "You will get a cramp."

"I haven't eaten, dear. Hadn't you noticed? And I would certainly cramp if I ate anything you cooked." Brother took off his clothes down to bathing trunks which he was wearing, folding each garment carefully and making a pile on the sand. In the pile between shirt and undershirt he placed the pistol. He walked across the beach into the surf and about thirty feet out took a graceful dive into a wave, beginning to swim lazily.

Doctor Englaster drank more brandy. "He is a little

more nasty than usual tonight, isn't he? I suppose he is beginning to feel all our waiting may not have been in vain, and perhaps that is good for his paranoia."

They ate in silence.

From time to time Harsh glanced at the small pile Brother's clothes made on the sand. "I wish he intended to use a bigger gun." He reached out casually to lift the shirt and expose the small automatic. He inspected it a few moments. Then he took his handkerchief from his coat pocket and used it to keep his fingers from touching the little gun as he picked it up. "I sure wouldn't want my prints on this thing." Harsh turned the gun back and forth, looking at it. It really was quite similar, he thought, to what he'd seen of the cop's in the back of the limousine. Not that he'd gotten that good a look in the heat of the moment, or a chance to give it a closer look since. "Twenty-five calibre, or twenty-two long rifle, one or the other. That shows how much I know about guns." He knew Mr. Hassam and Miss Muirz were watching him with a motionless poised attention that had come over them when he picked up the gun. "Me, I would want it larger." He put the gun back, picked up Brother's shirt and dropped it over the gun, replacing everything the way he had found it, except for the fact that he had swapped the cop's gun for that of Brother.

Harsh put his own handkerchief back in his pocket, Brother's gun going with it. Mr. Hassam and Miss Muirz relaxed enough to resume chewing food. They had not noticed, he decided. He had gotten away with it. Mr. Hassam and Miss Muirz would have said something if they had noticed the switch of guns, he was sure.

Harsh removed his coat and spread it over the pile of unused firewood to make a backrest, careful not to let the gun in the pocket clank against the wood. "Grub made me drowsy." He leaned back.

The two little automatics were remarkably alike. There had been no opportunity for a really close inspection to ascertain whether they were the same make, but they certainly looked similar enough to pass inspection at first glance.

And the important thing was, the one that could implicate him in a murder wasn't in his pocket anymore. If it wound up implicating Brother instead, well, Harsh thought, like they say, couldn't happen to a nicer guy.

The beach fire, down to coals, threw no more light than candles. Harsh wondered if it was enough light for Brother to notice any difference in the guns when he returned. He hoped not. But he could not relax, thinking of the risk.

Presently Brother came swimming in strongly from the ocean and ran to the fire, scattering drops of water. He put on his clothes over his wet body, breathing with deep animal-like regularity while he did so. He tucked the gun inside his shirt without more than a glance. Then he sat down cross-legged by the fire and began to eat ravenously.

Harsh looked at Mr. Hassam. "You said something about a talk."

"We have had it." Mr. Hassam sounded tired. "I merely wished to be sure you had grown more comfortable than the last time we spoke about it with the fact that there was eventually to be a murder."

"Was that all?"

"Yes."

Harsh stood up and stretched. "Then I'll see you folks in the morning. Okay?"

Mr. Hassam nodded. "I hope we have not said anything that will keep you from sleeping soundly."

"Don't worry about that. You knock off whoever you want to knock off, just so long as I get mine."

TWENTY

The whereabouts of the two automobiles was important. Harsh settled that point on his way to the house. The underslung sports car and the older station wagon were under the carport at the side of the house. He took a quick look at the driving controls of the sports car. They did not look complicated, he thought, but then Vera Sue wasn't the experienced driver he was. He began to worry about it.

The limousine was parked before the leaded glass marquee at the front door. He did not look inside, merely noted its position. As best he recalled, it was left there at night.

If anyone had found Goldberg's body, obviously something would have been mentioned.

The upstairs hallways smelled faintly of flowers, furniture polish. At the end of the hall the windows spilled rectangles of moonlight on dove grey carpet. The sound of a sob arrested him and he stood motionless, listening. Surf whispered distantly on the beach, the coyote sound of distant bathers was audible. Birds quarreled briefly somewhere in the shrubbery.

He opened Vera Sue Crosby's bedroom door. "For Christ's sake!" Vera Sue was lying on the bed with an arm over her face. She did not remove the arm when he sat on the edge of the bed. He leaned down, kissed her mouth, getting a slight taste of Benedictine off her lips. "What's the matter?"

She lifted the arm from her face, made a fist of her hand, and shook the fist angrily. "Stuck-up snobs, dirty bastards." Her face was puffy and her eye enraged. "Telling me I couldn't go down on the beach to eat with them."

"Say, did they do that? I didn't know they did that."

"Why don't you stick up for me, Walter?"

"I have been honey, but I didn't know about this."

She wiped her nose on the back of her hand. "You stick up for me, Walter? Crap."

"Honey, I do. I'm always thinking about you, you know that."

She sniffled moistly. "The way it looks to me, you do plenty of thinking about that Miss Muirz."

"Vera Sue, you want to know something, I'm scared of that dame." Harsh kissed her once more. This time she kissed back. "I'm getting scared of the whole bunch of them, if you want the facts."

"You follow them around like their puppy dog."

"I been playing them along. I thought I had them suckered into taking up my photographic emulsion idea and putting it over big."

Vera Sue sat up suddenly. "Walter! What the hell, are you trying to say your plans blew up?"

"Worse than that. Jesus Christ, worse than that." Harsh looked into the hall and closed the door before he came back to the bed. "You know what I found out tonight? These people are a bunch of crooks, that's what I found out tonight. And not our sort of crooks either."

"I ain't surprised." She was not tipsy in spite of the Benedictine on her lips. "I ain't surprised the least bit."

"Well, I was."

"Walter, the whole thing was too screwed up to be on the level. Couldn't you see that?" She peered at him intently. "Walter! My God, Walter, you *are* scared! I can see it on your face."

He nodded.

"Why? What have they done, Walter?"

"It's not what they've done, it's what they're planning to do. They're fixing up to murder a guy, put me in his place, and embezzle the guy's money. Damn right I'm scared. Wouldn't you be?"

He ran his fingers through his hair. "We got to be careful. They know I'm wise to their plans, and I got a feeling they won't want me walking out of here alive."

"Well, by God, I'm getting out. They don't think I know anything, do they?"

He shook his head. "I wouldn't put it past them to knock us both off. They're desperate characters. They ain't like Americans." He held his head in his hands, pretending to think. She was falling right in with his plans. "We got two handicaps, Vera Sue. No money. No transportation."

"Couldn't we take the limousine, then abandon it later, Walter?"

"Huh-uh, honey. No good. That little sports car could catch up with the limousine in nothing flat."

"Well, then what's wrong with taking the sports job?"

"Can you drive it?"

"I looked it over a few times, and once I sat in it. Yeah, I think I could handle it, Walter. But what the hell, you would be going along, and you could drive."

"What I was thinking, baby, you could take off by

yourself, and I would stay behind and fix the other cars so
they wouldn't run, then take off myself on foot. We could
meet later."

They were quiet. Harsh hoped the two servants were
on the main floor in the rear where they usually were this
time of the evening. He glanced out the bedroom window
and saw Mr. Hassam, Doctor Englaster, and Miss Muirz
still beside the beach fire with Brother.

"Walter. About the no money…?"

"Yeah?"

"I want to show you something." Vera Sue got off the
bed and moved to the door. "Walter, do you know anything about jewelry, whether it's worth anything or not by
looking at it?"

"What are you talking about?"

Vera Sue beckoned. "Come on. That Miss Muirz brought
some stuff with her when she came the last time. I been
doing a little snooping on my own, Walter. Come on, I
want to show you."

She drew Harsh down the hall and opened the door of
Miss Muirz's bedroom. "In these two suitcases." Her
voiced was husky with excitement. "Goddamn, if they're
real, Walter, we could come out of this with a stake."

The first suitcase she opened was packed with small
objects wrapped in tissue and cotton. She tore away the
wrappings, uncovering a necklace, several brooches, a
crown-like tiara. Diamonds, emeralds, platinum, the stones
all very large. Like owl eyes, Harsh thought.

"Jesus God, Vera Sue."

She fondled the jewel pieces. "You think they're real,
Walter? The other suitcase is full of the same stuff, too."

Excitement made the muscles ripple in her throat. "Is it costume jewelry, Walter, or the real McCoy?"

"It's real, baby."

"How do you know?"

"It figures. It belongs to the guy they're planning to kill. They already stole it from him, and he hasn't missed it yet, and won't ever miss it if they murder him. Yeah, it's got to be real. Say, if we take it and return it to the owner, we would be in line for a big reward."

"Reward? Return it?" Vera Sue looked startled. "Oh, well, sure, I see what you mean. Yeah, sure, Walter." She took a deep breath. "We don't have to hand it back to the owner right away, though, Walter, do you think?"

"No, of course not. We can keep it and negotiate with the owner, or his insurance company, so we don't get screwed out of a reward."

"Walter, how much reward do you suppose we would get?"

"Hell, how do I know? Maybe fifty thousand dollars. I don't know."

He saw her eyes turn all whites. He should not have mentioned a sum like that, he thought, remembering the effect fifty thousand dollars had had on him.

"Walter, get a bed sheet." Two spots of apple red grew on Vera Sue's cheeks. "We won't take the suitcases, they'd maybe be missed. We'll dump the stuff in a sheet."

He went to the door, listened, went out into the hall and silently on to Vera Sue's room, where he whipped the orchid sheet off the bed. He stowed it under his arm, ran back to join Vera Sue. She was on her knees beside the suitcase. "I just hope to Jesus this is not costume junk.

My God, maybe it's just a salesman's sample case of cheap trash."

"It's real, I'm betting on that."

She snatched the sheet from him and snapped it out shoulder height, guiding it to the floor with swaying motions of her upper body like a Bali dance. She dumped everything from both suitcases onto the sheet. Tissue paper, jewelry, cotton, everything. Her breath came and went in spurts past the tips of small white teeth. "I wish to hell we had something to stuff in the suitcases."

Harsh shook his head. "There's no time for that. They're right on the beach. We can't get much of a start as it is."

Vera Sue nodded reluctantly. "The first thing this Miss Muirz is going to do when she gets back inside is open the suitcases to gloat over the jewels. I know bitches like her, and I know that's what she'll do. And when she does, she's going to squall like a hill panther, and we had better be gone from here."

"All right. Let's go back to my plan. You take the sports car, Vera Sue. I'll put the other two cars out of commission and knock out the telephone, then take off north. That will split them up."

"The jewelry better go with me, Walter."

He stepped to her and without warning swung his fist. It landed on the side of her face. She slid to the floor with one leg folded under her and the other stretched out in front of her.

Harsh leaned over her. "That's to pay you for the god-damn greedy ideas I can see you're getting. You listen to me, baby. You double-cross me, you just try it, and what you just got is not even a small sample of what you got coming."

No more than the tips of small teeth showed between her lips. "It may be you just made a mistake, Walter."

"Like hell I just made a mistake. You try to cut me out of this deal, and I'll break your neck. Now listen. Go to a hotel in Miami. Register and wait for me. The way you pick a hotel, you look in the Yellow Pages. You look at the list of hotels and count down five from the first, and go to that one. If you can't get a room there, you make sure you leave a note for me. Say in the note where you did get a room. Fifth hotel down in the phone book, register or leave me a note. Got it?"

She drew in the leg that was straightened out and put the tips of her fingers on the floor. "You brutal son of a bitch. What do you think I am, stupid? I'm smarter than you, Walter. Least I can read and write better'n a ten-year-old."

"Okay. Okay, baby." He seized the bundle made of the knotted sheet and jewelry. "You want to play that way, I can take this stuff myself."

She jumped to her feet and snatched the bundle. "No, I'll do it. You just distract their attention while I get away." Her eyes glowed like angry garnets. "And I'll settle with you later for slugging me."

He opened the door and scouted the hall. "Come on." They walked along the hall and down the stairs. Vera Sue hugged the bundle tightly. The jewelry made rich faint scratching noises inside the sheet as it rubbed together.

Harsh led the way to the front door. When he opened it a current of air came from under the leaded marquee bearing the fragrance of azaleas.

Moonlight was cream-colored on the driveway and black shadows lurked in the shrubbery. Their feet whispered in the cropped grass. The toes of their shoes became shiny wet with dew.

"You are sure you can drive this thing, Vera Sue?" The sports car was a low shape in the moonlight, a pale powerhouse, sleek and opalescent like a pearl. He pushed Vera Sue down alongside the car and crouched himself. "You wait here. Don't let anybody see you sitting in the car. It will take a few minutes for me to disable the limousine and get that gate open. The gate will be the signal. When you see it open, take off. Cut loose and just keep going to Miami. I'll handle the rest."

"What about the station wagon, Walter?"

"I'll fix it now." He went over to the station wagon and opened the door and leaned inside. He did nothing but lean inside for a while, then went back to Vera Sue. "I tore the wires loose."

"Okay. I'll watch for the gate to open."

He leaned over her. "A kiss for luck?"

"Yes, Walter, you do deserve something for luck." She made a small hard fist of her hand and brought it against his nose, making the cartilage squeak like a pup's rubber mouse. "There, you bully. With my compliments."

He fell back and cupped his hand over his nose. "Okay. That's the one shot you get for free, baby. You try to steal this jewelry, I'll fix you good, Vera Sue. Let me be plain. You pull anything, you'd better sleep in a locked room every night after that, because the day you don't I'll find you and you'll never wake up."

"You're a nasty son of a bitch, Walter."

"You are so right. You just keep that in mind, baby."

Harsh returned to the house. Instead of going upstairs,

he entered the first floor study where there was a telephone. He held the instrument to his ear until he heard the dial tone to make sure it was an outside line, then he dialed the operator and told her he wanted the police. "The Highway Patrol. Emergency. Hurry, please." There was a pack of cigarettes on the table and he shook one out of the pack and put it in his mouth, but took it out quickly when he heard a female voice on the telephone. That a woman's voice should answer for the police surprised him. He was briefly confused, but recovered. "Highway Patrol?…Yeah, yeah, well listen. This is a tip-off. Two guys in a limousine. They got a body of a murdered man in the back. Black limousine, traveling south on the beach road right now. It will go west across the causeway, then south on U.S. 1. License plate's seven-zero-F-eight-zero-one. A murdered body in the back. Get on it."

"Who has been murdered?"

"He's dead as hell."

"Hold it a second." Harsh could hear the woman relaying the information. "What is your name, please?"

"Never mind my name. You think I'm crazy enough to get mixed up in this?" Harsh dropped the handset on the cradle.

He wondered if, when he hung up at his end, that broke the connection in the dialing apparatus so the call could not be traced. He wished he knew. At the same time he hoped he'd never find out. The time had come to get that money out of the wall safe and haul out of here.

He left the study after a glance from the window assured him that Mr. Hassam, Doctor Englaster, Miss Muirz, and Brother were still on the beach. They were

crouching around the portable radio with an attentive air,
like setters on point. Listening to another news broadcast, no doubt.

He went to his room and closed the door. He ripped
open the box which contained the slacks he had been
wearing when he shot the cop and dug his hand into the
pocket. He found the wall safe keys. The bits of metal felt
strange in his fingers. He stood there a moment with the
keys in his hand. He did not feel any immediate reaction
to holding them the way he had supposed he would.

He went to the wall safe and swung the oil painting
aside and worked the combination the first try. Got it first
crack, what do you know, he thought, and he made a little
celebratory ceremony of getting the two keys in the locks
in the inner door before turning either. The inner door
had no handle and the way it opened was by pulling on
the keys after they were turned, he imagined. He turned
the keys and tugged, bringing the door open. It was
exactly level with his eyes. The money was there.

He was looking right at fifty thousand dollars, he
thought, but he did not feel any particular elation. He
felt very calm, except that his ears seemed to have started
ringing. He drew out the money and divided it in two
halves and put each half in a pocket, one half in one hip
pocket and the other half in the other hip pocket. It was
funny how calm he felt, except that ringing in his ears.

Suddenly he bent over so he could clamp the hand
protruding from the cast to his left ear and his other hand
to his right ear. That stopped the ringing, shut it out. The
ringing was not in his ears. It was a bell somewhere in the
house. A burglar alarm, he thought, and he looked in the

safe and saw a little switch which closed a circuit when
the safe's inner door was opened. A goddamn burglar
alarm.

He wheeled and ran out of his room, down the stairs,
out of the house into the shrubbery. He tried to be silent
in the shrubbery shadows. Back of him the house was
huge and silent except for the alarm sounding. A breeze
rustled the palm fronds and rubbed the leaves against the
glass-crusted wall like insects running.

Harsh ran to the gate. Still unlocked, it swung open
silently as he shoved at it.

Now another bell jangled. Louder, nearer. The bastards got everything wired with alarms, he thought, and
he lunged into the shadows and began running toward
the carport. Breathing hard made his nose hurt. The gate
alarm was jangling, while the other had a muffled sound
as though it was being swallowed. He brushed a palm
tree, hurting his arm.

The sports car engine coughed and moaned and the
gears made a noise like screen wire tearing. Its headlights
thrust out white funnels of light, and these raced along
the driveway pursued by the powerful snarl of the engine.
The sports car shot past him and on through the gate.
Gravel torn up by the tires and thrown in the air fell back
on the driveway, grass, shrubbery.

Harsh reached the house. He saw Doctor Englaster,
Brother, Miss Muirz, and Mr. Hassam all running toward
him from the beach. Miss Muirz was well in the rear,
although she ran easily with a long loping stride. Must've
gotten a slower start.

Harsh cupped his hands to his mouth. "Hey, somebody! Vera Sue's beat it!" He ran toward the four coming from the beach. "That was Vera Sue in the sports car. Who the hell told her she could clear out?"

Brother ran toward the limousine. "Come! We must catch her."

Doctor Englaster piled into the limousine's passenger seat, next to Brother, who'd pulled the pistol out of his shirt and was gripping it tightly it in one hand.

Harsh gripped Mr. Hassam's arm. "Hold it!" He kept his voice low. "Don't go with them, for Christ's sake."

For a moment, Mr. Hassam pulled against Harsh's hand, turning to give Harsh a strange look. Suddenly he grunted in comprehension.

"You two go on!" Mr. Hassam waved at the pair in the limousine. "We'll follow in the station wagon. We can search more roads with two cars."

Miss Muirz arrived, and Harsh had the sudden feeling that she'd hung back on purpose, that she could have outrun any of them from the beach if she had wanted to but had held back out of caution. She was moving swiftly now toward the limousine's rear door as it began pulling away. Moving even more swiftly, Mr. Hassam tripped her. She went down on the grass.

"Go on! Hurry!" Mr. Hassam's bellow was directed at Brother and Doctor Englaster in the limousine.

The limousine had twin exhaust pipes. Blue smoke coughed out of both of these along with a powerful sound. The tires spun and shoveled gravel backward, and the limousine raced out of view through the gate.

TWENTY-ONE

Harsh watched the limousine vanish and inhaled with relief. Now if the Highway Patrol was on the job, the matter of the cop's murder would be up to Brother and Doctor Englaster to explain. Brother was carrying the gun with which the cop had been killed and driving the man's body down the highway at top speed. Even if Doctor Englaster was only mildly tipsy rather than out-and-out drunk, giving him better control of his faculties and his tongue, he wouldn't have an easy time explaining the situation to the police, Harsh thought.

Miss Muirz, sitting on the grass, looked at Mr. Hassam, who was still eyeing Harsh curiously. "You tripped me."

"Yes." Mr. Hassam did not deny it. A thin line of blood was coming from his lower lip where a piece of driveway gravel must have hit it when the limousine was departing.

"Why?" Miss Muirz's voice was bell clear.

Mr. Hassam started toward the carport. "If we are going to follow, we had better get going."

Miss Muirz moved swiftly. She was the first one to the station wagon. "I'll drive." She started the engine. "Meanwhile, you can answer my question."

She was a sharp one, Harsh thought, and a fast one when the chips began to fall. She knew something had gone wrong, and she was moving right to the front to find out what it was. Better stay close to this babe, he told himself, or she may manage to gum up the works.

He got into the station wagon and Mr. Hassam slid

into the rear seat beside him, fell back with him against the cushion and struggled to get the door closed as the car got underway.

Miss Muirz was through all three forward gears before the station wagon reached the gate. "So. Why." Her voice was even more calm, more bell-like. "Why did you stop me from going with Brother and Doctor Englaster?"

Mr. Hassam winced as they grazed the gate. "I was afraid to ride with Brother. I thought you would be also, if you had time to stop and think. Do you blame me?"

"You lie at the wrong times, Achmed." Some distance ahead on the blacktop beach road there was a fast-moving bloom of light with two red taillights embedded in the lower center. "That was not why you tripped me, Achmed."

The blob of light ahead suddenly skated right and left as the road made an S curve. "That was not why you tripped me, Achmed. Right?"

The ribbon of blood from Mr. Hassam's lip reached his chin, a drop fell on his hand, and he looked down at it in amazement.

"Well, I had some advice." He reached for his handkerchief and applied it to his mouth. "It aroused a cooperative feeling toward you, Miss Muirz. I hope I did not act in error."

"Advice? Indeed?"

"Yes." Mr. Hassam's handkerchief muffled his voice somewhat. "It came from Mr. Harsh here. I presume you'd want to know that."

"What?" Miss Muirz had not understood.

"Mr. Harsh told me to stay out of the limousine, and I included you." Mr. Hassam lowered the handkerchief.

The station wagon negotiated the S curve and they were thrown to one side and then the other. "What are you pulling on us, Harsh?" Miss Muirz's voice rang loudly.

"Jesus, slow down, will you!" Harsh had been weighing the quality of Miss Muirz's driving, and he was sure they would hold their own with the limousine, if not overtake it. "You don't want to catch that limousine." If they came up with the limousine as the police stopped it, there might be complications. He shouted over the roar of motor and wind, "Slow down! For Christ's sake."

"Why?" Miss Muirz did not turn her head.

"I got a damn good reason."

Ahead of them the limousine lights suddenly disappeared around a turn. Miss Muirz did not slacken their headlong speed. Harsh held his breath. He felt Miss Muirz would go into the turn wide open. Mr. Hassam thought so too, and he grabbed onto the door handle. "A turn! Watch it!"

Miss Muirz's voice was too high-pitched, too composed. "I will do the driving." She braked and went into the turn with all tires shrieking; in a moment they were straightened out, headed for the causeway and bridge.

"Oh, God." Mr. Hassam had clamped his handkerchief over his forehead.

Harsh saw there was no question they were gaining on the limousine. Desperation made his mouth dry. He took out Brother's automatic pistol and brandished it over the back of Miss Muirz's seat. "Slow down, goddamn it, I don't want to have to shoot anybody."

Miss Muirz ignored the gun. "At this speed, shoot the driver? You are a fool, but not that big a fool." She apparently had no concern about the gun.

Mr. Hassam, however, had plenty. His eyes flew wide and he clutched the door handle again. "Harsh! That gun! Where did you get Brother's gun?"

Miss Muirz was crowding the centerline of the road. "Relax, Achmed. At this speed, he will not shoot anyone."

"That's not the point." Mr. Hassam did not take his eyes off the little automatic. "That can't be Brother's gun. He had his gun in his hand when he got in the limousine." Mr. Hassam's voice rose. "But it looks exactly like Brother's gun. How in God's name, Harsh? What's going on?"

"I took a gun off a guy who got killed." Harsh's voice shook. He was frightened by the insane driving. "I got the guy's gun out of his pocket, swapped it for Brother's on the beach."

They were well out on the dike-like causeway leading to the bridge, with the moon-bathed water of the Indian River rushing past on either side. The limousine lights were still well ahead and beyond the bridge. As yet there was no sign of Vera Sue in the pearl-colored sports car.

"What guy, Harsh?" Hassam's voice was frantic. "What are you talking about?"

And still Miss Muirz had not slowed down at all.

"You want to know what I'm talking about? There's a corpse in that limousine. Do you hear me?" Harsh pounded desperately on the back of the driver's seat. "This guy I killed, his body's in the back of the limousine. The Highway Patrol has been tipped off to stop the limousine. Now, goddamn it, will you slow down? You want us all in jail?"

The bridge rushed at them like a mouth of steel girders preparing to snap them up. It was an old-fashioned bridge with a tall black mesh of ironwork and a slight rise in the pavement at the entrance. The station wagon took off from this rise with a jerk downward at their bellies, then a long sensation of flying in space, and the shock of landing. The bridge passed them with a coughing sound, spat them out on the other side.

"A body in the limousine?" Mr. Hassam gripped Harsh's arm. "Man, are you making that up? Is it true?"

"It's true."

"Who did you murder, Harsh?"

"I didn't *murder* him." Far ahead Harsh could distinguish a cluster of lights that would be the U.S. 1 intersection. "The guy got killed, sure, but it was an accident. He was a guy who was snooping around the car—a cop, I think. I had this locksmith in town make me a duplicate key for the wall safe, and this cop somehow got wind of it. This afternoon I was supposed to meet the locksmith to get the key while you were looking at suits in Leon's, but when I went outside, it was the cop waiting in the limousine. He was all bundled up to disguise himself but I recognized him from the day before. And to be honest, I think he recognized me, too—he seemed to know my face, anyway, and seemed sort of shocked to see it. And he was full of questions, like what were we plotting—that was the word he used—and when I wouldn't answer his questions, he tried to pull his gun on me. Then we scrapped over the gun, and he got shot. I left his body in the limousine and took his gun, the one that killed him, and on the beach I traded it for the one Brother packed. The reason I swapped them, the guns looked a lot alike to me, that's all. I figured it was too good an opportunity to pass up. Better Brother gets nabbed with the murder weapon than me, right? Then to make sure he did get nabbed, I fixed up the rest, tipped the Highway Patrol to grab the limousine. And that's why I didn't want you to get in that car. Not with a dead man in the back."

Looking over, Harsh saw that Mr. Hassam had a horrified expression on his face. "Harsh, the gun Brother had in his hand just now, when he got into the limousine…it didn't just look similar, it looked identical. And it's not a gun you can buy just anywhere. It's only made custom, for collectors."

Suddenly the station wagon went nearly out of control. Two wheels left the pavement, and it rocked crazily, bounced off a curb, began to skate from side to side. Mr. Hassam yelled and flung himself forward, reaching over both the driver's seat and Miss Muirz's shoulders to seize the steering wheel and straighten them out.

Miss Muirz spoke over the roar of engine and tires. "Thank you, Achmed. Now I can handle it." Her voice was even more odd than before.

The limousine, traveling very fast into the intersection ahead, now had all four wheels locked with the brakes, and it was veering slowly broadside in a skid. It was not out of control, however, because suddenly it shot south out of the intersection.

Harsh muttered close to Mr. Hassam's ear. "What's the matter with Miss Muirz? I thought she was gonna wreck us."

"Don't you know who you killed, Harsh?"

"Sure, some cop who was on our tail."

"No." Mr. Hassam shook his head heavily. "No, it was *El Presidente*."

o

A Highway Patrol car moved southward out of a service station at the highway intersection, gathering speed, siren going, winking two red spotlights.

Moments later, the station wagon approached the intersection. There were four large gasoline service stations, one at each corner, each adorned with vari-colored neon lighting, and the effect was somewhat like plunging toward a miniature sunrise.

With a stomach-wrenching shock, Miss Muirz threw on the brakes and sent the station wagon into the same kind of skid the limousine had made. The car yawed wildly. Harsh and Mr. Hassam were pitched against the front seat, their breath driven from them. Harsh closed his eyes for the crash…

However the station wagon, with a hard thrust from the engine, recovered in the turn and veered south. Harsh got a glimpse of pale scared faces watching them from the service stations. The police car and the limousine were ahead. And he got, for the first time, a brief glimpse of the pearl-colored sports car farther on.

"Oh, Jesus!" Harsh pushed himself back on the seat. "I thought we were goners." He tried to lick his lips and found his tongue felt numb. "What was that you said before we hit the corner?"

"You killed *El Presidente*, Harsh." Mr. Hassam's voice was shrill with shock and nervousness.

"Nah, it couldn't be. I tell you it was a cop, some guy hired to snoop around."

"No. I am sure. The guns are identical."

"So what? Factories all make guns of the same model alike."

"I tell you, these are custom made, the only ones of

their type. I'd recognize them anywhere. They were a
diplomatic gift to *El Presidente* years ago. His brother
took one, but he retained the other. Both men have always
kept them." Hassam reached out a hand, palm up. "The
Uruguayan ambassador had *El Presidente's* initials engraved on the underside of the butt. Look for yourself if
you won't hand it over."

"One of us is nuts." But Harsh turned the gun in his
hand, and with a terrible sinking feeling saw the mono-
gram engraved on the bottom.

"Look!" Miss Muirz's voice was a bell pealing out
horror. "Gunfire!"

The Highway Patrol was traveling very fast. On the
right side just under where the spotlight was mounted,
muzzle flame from a firearm was winking redly.

Beyond the patrol car, the limousine veered slowly to
the left and began riding the highway shoulder; it rode
the shoulder a short distance. It had been hit by the gunfire. Suddenly, like a running animal scared off its path, it
plunged into a field. The limousine abruptly vaulted into
the air, swapping ends as it went, the headlight hurling
bursts of brilliance about like lightning flashes. Then the
headlights suddenly went out and it was dark in the field.

The Highway Patrol car overran the spot where the
limousine had left the road. It went on about two hundred yards before it halted.

The pearl-colored sports car, ignored by everyone,
went on and soon its lights were no longer discernible.

TWENTY-TWO

Miss Muirz brought the station wagon to a stop. It stood on the highway just about where the limousine had left to go tumbling into the adjacent field. A soft and fragrant breeze cooled their faces and around them it had become very quiet. The Highway Patrol car, which was backing up, seemed in no hurry. Harsh suppressed an urge to get out of the station wagon. Mr. Hassam was leaning back on the seat with his face upraised and his mouth wide open.

Miss Muirz's hands moved slowly as if caressing the steering wheel rim while she stared straight ahead at nothing.

"Well, I guess we're all in one piece." Harsh cleared his throat. "I never thought we would make it." He looked at the approaching police car. "You people are crazy to stay parked here, you know that don't you?"

Mr. Hassam exhaled heavily and held out his hand again to Harsh. "Give me the gun. We must prevent *El Presidente's* body from being identified."

"Are you nuts?" Harsh pushed his hand away. "The cops got their eye on us right now. That's why they're backing up so slow."

The Highway Patrol car swung sharply and came to a stop crosswise on the highway pavement a few yards ahead of the station wagon, blocking the way. There were two officers in the patrol car. One alighted, service revolver in hand, and approached carefully.

"You folks get out and lie on the ground." The officer sounded very nervous. "Whoever's in that car that just went off the road is armed. They were shooting at us." There was the web-like pattern of a bullet hole in the Highway Patrol car windshield.

Harsh spoke quietly. "Okay, officer. We just stopped to see what had happened. We didn't know what was going on."

The patrolman stepped toward Harsh, his eyes narrowing. "Do I know you? Your face looks familiar."

At that moment, the officer who had remained in the patrol car switched on a spotlight. It produced a long white rod of light with which he poked about in the adjacent field until he found the limousine. "Hey, Dick, look!" The wreck lay about sixty yards off the highway.

Everyone stared at the wreck. Harsh felt he would not have recognized the jumble of metal as the limousine had he not known better.

The patrolman standing beside the station wagon called out to the officer in their car. "Nobody in that thing is gonna do any more shooting." He crossed the highway and went down into the grader ditch. He moved sidewise going down and dug his heels in so he would not slide. He jumped over some water in the bottom of the ditch and went on toward what was left of the limousine. The other officer followed him.

Harsh felt of his pockets, making sure he still had the money from the wall safe. "Let's get the hell out of here. Before they come back."

Mr. Hassam shook his head. "No. Not without the body of *El Presidente*."

"You're nuts, Hassam. That body is a cop. Maybe he

got hold of *El Presidente's* gun somehow, but it couldn't be *El Presidente*. You heard the radio, *El Presidente* is on a gunboat in the harbor down there in South America."

"A false scent." Mr. Hassam's voice was bitter. "He suspected us, and he came here to spy on us. You remember we thought a car was trailing you and Miss Muirz a few nights ago? Well, one was, evidently, and no doubt it was *El Presidente*."

"How would he know where to look for you?"

"You think he couldn't find out where Brother's estate is? He must have been watching it for days, following us any time we went out."

"Okay, but why would he jump on me, try to kill me? You four, sure, but me, I'm nobody to him."

"Nobody is the last thing you were to him, Harsh— and if you'd looked in a mirror lately you'd know why. The first time he saw you he must have thought *he* was looking in a mirror. Even with that bandage on your face, he'd have immediately known something was up."

Harsh frowned, then remembered something. "I know how to settle this. I took his wallet. The dead man's. That'll tell us who he was." He felt hurriedly in his pockets. "I ain't had time to look at it. Here."

Mr. Hassam seized the billfold. "A passport case." He ignored some paper currency. "Ah! God!" Mr. Hassam closed his eyes tightly. "It was *El Presidente*. It is his passport."

"I don't believe it!" Harsh seized the case and examined the passport. His hands began to shake. "Christ, let's clear out of here. They find the body of an ex-president in that car, even a South American one, and there's going to be a tall stink. What are we waiting on?"

A low mewing sound came from Miss Muirz. It startled Harsh, chilling his nerves, and he looked at her. But Miss Muirz had not moved.

The two Highway Patrolmen reached the wreckage of the limousine. They began shining their flashlight beams about in it.

Mr. Hassam started toward the spot where the limousine had careened off the road. "Come. You and I will get the body now."

Harsh drew back. "The hell with you, buddy. I want out of here, is all I want."

Mr. Hassam's voice was soft, but suddenly very ugly. "Harsh, you have fifty thousand dollars in your pockets. I know, because I heard the alarm begin ringing when you opened the safe. I know that you feel you have a fortune in your pockets. But you listen to me, Harsh, listen closely. If you leave here now, you are running out on a chance to share in real money. *El Presidente* has nearly sixty-five million dollars on deposit in various institutions. You can impersonate him, and Miss Muirz's handwriting has already forged his name on all the deposit documents. Can you conceive of the sum sixty-five million? You cannot, can you, Harsh? You really cannot. The piddling sum of fifty thousand made you sick at your stomach."

One of the Highway Patrolmen got on his knees and threw his flashlight beam into the entrails of the wreck.

Harsh's mouth had gone dry. "This is the first time anybody said anything to me about a share in sixty-five million."

"Naturally. Why mention it when you were hysterically happy with fifty thousand?"

The Highway Patrolman put his flashlight on the ground and began to pull at something inside the wreck with his hands.

Mr. Hassam spoke grimly. "If that is *El Presidente's* body he is pulling out of there, we are lost."

"You think if we can keep the body from being identified, we can still grab everything?"

"Why not?"

The patrolman drew his hands out of the wreckage and hurriedly wiped them on the ground.

"All right." Harsh hardly recognized his own voice. "Let's get the body."

Miss Muirz made the odd mewing sound again. As before, there was no indication she had moved.

"Jesus!" Alarmed, Harsh looked back at Miss Muirz, who still hadn't gotten out of the station wagon. Her face was immobile and expressionless. The features could have been cut in glass. As he looked at her, her hands began to caress the wheel rim slowly, and he realized she had been doing that off and on since they had stopped. "What's wrong with her, Hassam?"

"Let her alone." Mr. Hassam leaned close to Miss Muirz. "We are going after the body, Mr. Harsh and I. Do you understand, Miss Muirz?"

A tremor went through her, but the even rhythm with which her hands stroked the steering wheel rim was not altered.

Mr. Hassam turned and crossed the pavement. "Come, Harsh." He went down the embankment and hesitated at the bottom, frowning at the water in the ditch. "Footprints in the mud. We must be careful of them." The ditch water was black in the moonlight.

Harsh jerked his head in the direction of the station wagon. "What's her problem?"

"Shock." Mr. Hassam prepared to jump the ditch. "*El Presidente* is dead. She was his mistress for twenty years."

"Oh." Harsh had not supposed Miss Muirz to be much more than thirty years of age now.

Mr. Hassam read his thought. "*El Presidente* always liked them young." He sprang at the ditch, landing in the mud and water with a splash. He swore, kicked his feet to throw off the loose mud.

They climbed up a slope toward the wrecked limousine. The two patrolmen, intent on what the interior of the wreck held, did not notice their approach at first. One officer said something to his companion and both ran around to the other side of the wreck.

Mr. Hassam's whisper was firm and unafraid. "I will tell the officers I am a doctor, and the body is alive, and must be rushed to a hospital. Using that excuse, we will make off with it."

"I hope they fall for it. It's a good idea."

At least fifty feet away from the wreck the reek of raw gasoline was pronounced. Harsh stumbled over an object and looked down and saw the object was a wheel with the tire still in place on it, the wheel almost entirely embedded in the soft earth. At closer view, the limousine looked even less like an automobile than it had appeared from the road.

Nearby palm trees with tall silver trunks leaned forward like inquiring sentries.

"Dick, watch it!" One patrolman drew his revolver. "Oh, it's the people from the station wagon." He raised his voice irritably. "I thought I told you folks to stay on the road."

Mr. Hassam strode forward. "I am a doctor. Someone here may need medical care."

"Well, okay." There was quite a lot of dark blood on the patrolman's hands. "There's three bodies in there, it looks like. But it's a mess."

Harsh tried to sound calm. "Doc and I will do what we can." He peered into the tangle of steel, wishing he had a flashlight.

The reek of gasoline was overpowering. Harsh could hear it still trickling from a hole in the tank. He was appalled. He had not imagined an automobile could be reduced to such a shapeless thing—even D.C. Roebuck's hadn't been mangled quite this thoroughly. He thrust his right arm into what had been the rear seat section.

"If anybody's alive, it's in front." The patrolman sounded impatient.

"I saw something move." Harsh was lying. His groping fingers had encountered cold flesh that was firm to the touch. "Doc!"

Mr. Hassam got down beside him. "The body?" Mr. Hassam's whisper was flat and without emotion.

"Yes." Harsh decided he had hold of an arm. He pulled with all his strength. "Damn thing won't budge." He began to pant.

Mr. Hassam also seized the body's arm, and they both tugged with all their might. The body would not move.

The patrolmen were working on the other side of the wreck. They were yanking and kicking at the twisted metal.

Mr. Hassam's lips were against Harsh's ear. "It's wedged. A knife! Have you a knife?"

"No. Why?"

"I want to cut off the head and hands."

"No, I ain't got a knife." Harsh's stomach did not feel well.

Both the patrolmen abruptly stood erect. They were looking in the direction of the highway. One lifted his voice. "Hey, lady! Lady, you stay back. Don't come down here."

Miss Muirz was coming toward them from the station wagon. She had crossed the ditch and she walked jerkily as if propelled by clockwork. She was looking straight ahead as she came. Her trim legs wore their coating of mud nearly to the knees, like boots.

"Go back, lady! Stay away!" The patrolman waved both arms urgently. "This'll just make you sick. Go back!"

Miss Muirz had both hands clasped together before her breasts, and Harsh suddenly realized she had a revolver in her hands. Mr. Hassam realized this also. The patrolman had not noticed the gun.

"Gotta stop her!" Harsh hurried forward, Mr. Hassam on his heels, and they put themselves between Miss Muirz and the officers before the latter could see the revolver.

Miss Muirz did not seem to have any awareness of Harsh and Mr. Hassam standing in her path. Her progress ended only when she collided with Mr. Hassam, and even then she continued to stare vacantly in the same direction she had been staring as she walked. Mr. Hassam gripped her shoulders and held them.

"Harsh, go back, use a piece of broken window glass, cut off the hands and head." Mr. Hassam still seemed calm.

"Won't work. The cops got their eyes on us." Harsh's teeth chattered together. "Listen, I got an idea. The whole wreck is soaked with gasoline. I'm gonna pretend to light a cigarette, drop the match. That'll burn the bodies."

Miss Muirz's body was rigidly inclined against Mr. Hassam as if she were still trying to walk.

"All right, Harsh."

Harsh ran back to the wreck. One of the patrolmen looked up from the wreck. "So you got the woman headed off? Good. This would be a bad thing for her to see."

"Yeah. She's okay."

The beams from the flashlights the patrolmen held were glistening on gasoline wetness throughout the wreckage. Harsh thought the fuel tank must have split wide open when the limousine was somersaulting. "How are you guys making out?"

The patrolman shrugged. "Three of them. All dead, near as we can tell."

"I'm gonna work on the other side, officer." Harsh moved around the wreckage, feeling for a cigarette. Then he realized he had no cigarettes. However he had matches, and if the officers did not see him, he could claim he had dropped his cigarette in his excitement when the wreck caught fire. They might or might not believe that, but they'd have no way to prove it wasn't so.

He found a match and struck it. The flame leaped with

unexpected brightness in his face. The patrolmen were not looking. He dropped the burning match in the wreckage quickly.

A blast of flame enveloped him. His clothing was ablaze. He had, he realized with horror, underestimated the explosive violence of gasoline vapor. He stumbled back. He had also forgotten he had been squirming around in the gasoline-drenched wreckage trying to get the body out. Jesus, he thought, I'm burning like a torch.

Mr. Hassam turned his head when the wreckage mushroomed in flame, and he squinted into the enormous mass that was the wreck, then saw a smaller violently moving bundle of flames that he knew must be Harsh. The stupid fool, Mr. Hassam thought. He could see Harsh was clawing and slapping at the flames with his arms, both the arm in a cast and the one that was not. The cast itself was in flames, too, and so was the bandage on Harsh's face, which fell off in cinders as he watched. Mr. Hassam suddenly felt tired. Everything had been working so perfectly; now it was in such a mess. Everything was black and white like that. With an impersonator to stand in for *El Presidente* they could have looted the hidden funds; without such an impersonator there would be no chance. A few hours ago Harsh had been in good condition and cooperating; now Harsh had stupidly thrown everything away. The stupid fool, the utterly stupid fool.

Also Mr. Hassam felt concern about Miss Muirz. He could tell she was in deep shock, her contact with reality badly disrupted. He was not really surprised; Miss Muirz's

emotional existence for some twenty years had been tied
to the man she had suddenly learned was dead, his body
now burning in the wrecked limousine. Mr. Hassam and
Doctor Englaster had discussed Miss Muirz's emotional
ties with *El Presidente* previously; they had determined
to insulate her as much as possible from the murder
when it was done. But everything had gotten out of hand,
thanks to the idiot Harsh. There was really nothing much
he could do about it, was there?

It was then that Miss Muirz shot him exactly in the
heart.

The two Highway Patrolmen had stumbled backward
when the flame spurted and had turned and were running to get clear. They halted at the sound of the shot.

Harsh also heard the shot with which Miss Muirz killed
Mr. Hassam. But he thought at first it was something
exploding in the flaming wreck. Perhaps the bullets in
the gun carried by Brother had started letting go in the
heat. In a corner of his mind he wondered whether the
heat would damage the gun barrel so the ballistics men
could not verify that it had fired the bullet that had killed
the body in the back seat.

He was rather proud of himself, being able to think
out the matter of heat damage to Brother's gun while
flames were seething in his clothes. Didn't they say a man
always lost his head when he caught fire? Well, he wasn't
losing his.

The flames were not yet actually charring his clothing.
They still fed on the gasoline vapor that came from the
cloth, blue devils darting here and there. The heat,

though, was almost unbearable. He kept beating at the flames, and he tried to brush off individual tongues of flame, but without much success.

He turned in the direction the sound of the gunshot had come from. He saw Miss Muirz, the revolver in her hand. She'd had a gun in that purse of hers, he remembered. She was coming toward him. She stumbled over something on the ground, but did not fall. She did not look down to see what had impeded her progress, although it was Mr. Hassam. In a moment flame and noise came Harsh's direction from Miss Muirz's gun. She had not aimed the gun, merely pulled the trigger. But the bullet barely missed him; he could feel it fan the side of his face. She held her gun out before her with both hands, still not aiming, but pointing more accurately. From the muzzle, flame, noise. Harsh stumbled back, not hit, dodging wildly. Half mad with pain he went for the automatic in his pocket. Miss Muirz came on. She measured her steps like a farmer pacing a field. He got the automatic out of his pocket. He shot her. Luck was with him. He got her almost exactly between the eyes, almost as precisely as a moment before she had placed her own bullet in Mr. Hassam's heart.

Both of the patrolmen had by now circled the burning limousine and they rushed Harsh. One knocked Harsh down with a fist. The other kicked the little gun away. They tore off Harsh's burning clothing in strips, cooling their scorched hands by slapping them against their thighs. They got the charred shirt off. Each officer seized a trouser leg. They pulled. Harsh was dragged a short distance, then the trousers came off. The moment the trousers were off, they blazed up furiously. The officer tossed them aside.

"Jesus Christ, save the pants!" Harsh struggled to reach the burning trousers. "My money's in them pants, Jesus Christ!"

An officer kicked Harsh backwards and he fell to the ground. The officer put his foot on Harsh's throat and leaned on it with most of his weight. He had his own gun drawn now and he aimed it down at Harsh. "You're under arrest."

TWENTY-THREE

After Harsh had been in the hospital nine days, he was removed from the hospital and placed in jail. The inquest had been held while he was in the hospital, and they had taken him somewhere on a litter for his share of that, but he did not remember much about it. Just some stuff about five people dead, an automobile crash and some shooting. Then some words he did not know, such as extradition. Harsh lay on the litter swathed in burn dressings. His mind was relaxed from the dope they had shot into him to ease the pain of the burns. He had not cared much what happened.

When he had been in jail three days, Vera Sue Crosby paid him a visit. With Vera Sue was a solidly built man with a heavy face and foxy eyes. He sat near Vera Sue back of the glass window in the interview room. There was no opening in the glass panel between Harsh and Vera Sue, only a mechanical diaphragm that passed their voices back and forth.

"Who's this bird?" Harsh did not like the looks of the heavy-bodied man.

"This is Mr. Arnick, my attorney." Vera Sue was wearing new clothes, a crisp grey tropical suit and she had a fresh permanent.

Harsh swallowed nervously. "Is he going to represent me, too?"

Lawyer Arnick shook his head. "I think not. Miss Crosby

happens to be my client, and your interests and her interests are not exactly identical."

"What does that mean, shyster?"

Vera Sue leaned toward the diaphragm in the glass panel which separated them. "You listen to me. I waited in that hotel in Miami. But you didn't show up. Then I heard about Mr. Arnick being a good attorney from a fellow I had a few drinks with, and I went to see Mr. Arnick. We had a nice talk and I hired him."

Harsh looked at her bitterly. "You split the jewelry with him to pay him for keeping you out of it. That right?"

Lawyer Arnick cleared his throat. "There was no jewelry." His eyes glittered over a faint smile. "We never heard of any jewelry."

Vera Sue nodded. "That's right."

"God almighty." Harsh felt the life draining out of him. "You can't do that, you got to help me, Vera Sue."

She smoothed the new tropical suit with her hands. "From what I hear tell, nobody can help you. Not where you're going.

"What do you mean?"

Arnick leaned forward. "Surely you must have heard. They're going to extradite you to South America to stand trial in your own country."

"My own—"

Arnick smiled smugly. "For crimes against the state and against your people."

"My people! What are you talking about? Who do you think I am?" The answer dawned on him as he shouted the question. "No. No—I'm Walter Harsh. I'm Walter Harsh! Vera Sue, tell him. Tell him who I am!"

"Everyone knows who you are," Vera Sue said. "It's been on all the television stations the past two weeks. I don't see how you could expect anyone to believe you're someone else—your Excellency." There was the faintest hint of a smile on her lips before she spoke the last two words, but she erased it as quickly as it had come.

"No, you can't do this, Vera Sue. *El Presidente's* body, it was in the car—"

Arnick cut him off. "Maybe you should ask them to bring you the newspapers for the last few days. Then you would know that all the bodies in the car were burned beyond recovery or recognition. Your own burns were quite serious, too, I understand—but not to a comparable degree, and they didn't prevent your identity from being conclusively established. Your facial scar, fingerprint records, dental records, the passport you were carrying, the monogrammed gun. Even down to your blood type, O-negative—not exactly common, you know."

Harsh felt his throat closing up.

"Don't do this, Vera Sue. Don't let them do this. You know who I am."

She stood up. Her voice when she spoke was low and vicious. "Sure, I know who you are. You're a nasty son of a bitch. How could I forget that?"

Harsh watched Lawyer Arnick take her arm and they walked away together. He was sure he would never see her again.

The cell window through which the intense South American sun poured in had four bars on it. But the figure four did not fit in with anything else. Harsh lay on the bunk and tried to associate the figure four with something,

with anything, but without success. The digit did not fit
in with anything, it did not fit in with fifty thousand dollars which had burned, nor with sixty-five million, nor did
it fit with seven, the number of people involved, Mr.
Hassam and Doctor Englaster and Brother and Miss
Muirz and *El Presidente* and Vera Sue and himself. Ten
persons if you counted D. C. Roebuck and the two house
servants at Brother's place, or twelve if you included the
two Highway Patrolmen who had arrested him, thirteen
if you threw in the judge down here who had sentenced
him to hang. Thirteen was a hot number. He guessed he
would have to throw in Attorney Arnick and make it four-
teen. There, he finally had something with four in it.

One thing for damn sure, he thought, Mr. Hassam had
been wrong. Mr. Hassam had told him that he could
never grasp how much sixty-five millions was, could not
grasp such magnitude. Well, Hassam had been dead
wrong, because Harsh could figure out how much sixty-
five millions was. He could do that, all right. If he paid
out one dollar for each breath he took, that would be
paying out about fifteen dollars a minute, wouldn't it? He
counted his own breathing through what he estimated to
be one minute. He timed the minute by counting chim-
panzees the way he did in the photographic darkroom,
"One chimpanzee, two chimpanzee," and so on. One
minute, fifteen breaths. All the minutes in one hour were
sixty, which times fifteen was nine hundred dollars an
hour. That times twenty-four for one day, that was how
much? Nine hundred times twenty-four was twenty-one
thousand and six hundred dollars. That was one day. In
dollars. All the days in the year were three hundred and
sixty-five if you didn't screw around with leap year, and

this times twenty-one thousand and six hundred dollars per day was still only, what, seven or eight million? He lay back. His breath came and went with such dryness it parched his lips. So sixty-five million was all the breaths you could take in five, six, seven, eight years, with change left over. It was a lot of honey for no one to taste, ever. That was sure.

If he had it, maybe he could use it to buy those eight years. But he didn't have it, not a penny of it, and he didn't have any eight years either. Or eight months or eight weeks or eight days. Outside the cell window he heard the stamping feet of the *descamisada*, the shirtless ones. He remembered enough of the Spanish Mr. Hassam had taught him to know they were calling for his blood.

Eight *minutes*—how much would that cost? He counted desperately on his fingers. Hundred twenty dollars. It would take four or five sales calls with his camera to earn that. His camera. He wondered what had become of it.

Eight seconds? Could he even buy eight seconds more of life? It would only cost a dime or so. One thin dime. Surely he had that much on him somewhere!

He was still feeling of his pockets when they came to his cell to collect him.

THE
END

More Fine Books From
HARD CASE CRIME!

The Gutter and the Grave
by ED McBAIN
MWA GRANDMASTER

Detective Matt Cordell was happily married once, and gainfully employed, and sober. But that was before he caught his wife cheating on him with one of his operatives.

The Guns of Heaven
by PETE HAMILL
ACCLAIMED JOURNALIST

Terrorists from Northern Ireland plan to strike in New York City—and only one newspaper reporter stands in their way.

Night Walker
by DONALD HAMILTON
CREATOR OF 'MATT HELM'

When Navy lieutenant David Young came to in a hospital bed, his face was covered with bandages and the nurses were calling him by a stranger's name...

Available now at your favorite bookstore.
For more information, visit
www.HardCaseCrime.com